A SMALL MADNESS

A SMALL MADNESS

•

DIANNE TOUCHELL

Groundwood Books
House of Anansi Press
Toronto / Berkeley

Groundwood Books / House of Anansi Press
groundwoodbooks.com

With the participation of the Government of Canada | Canadä
Avec la participation du gouvernement du Canada

Library and Archives Canada Cataloguing in Publication
Touchell, Dianne, author
A small madness / Dianne Touchell.
Issued in print and electronic formats.
ISBN 978-1-55498-837-2 (bound) — ISBN 978-1-55498-839-6 (html). —
ISBN 978-1-55498-840-2 (mobi)
I. Title.
PZ7.T672Sm 2016   j823'.92   C2015-904612-2
C2015-904613-0

Jacket design and illustration and interior design by Michael Solomon

Groundwood Books is committed to protecting our natural environment.
As part of our efforts, the interior of this book is printed on paper that contains
100% post-consumer recycled fibers, is acid-free and is processed chlorine-free.

Printed and bound in Canada

For Ainslie Harris Touchell

1

He'd eaten an orange. His fingers were sticky with it and smelled strongly of that pith muck that collects under your fingernails after you peel the rind off.

She didn't care. They were in love. She let him put his sticky hands in places her own had never been. All those places she'd been warned about. The places that attracted strangers with lost puppies and the wrong touch and sin. Private places that embarrassed her and shocked her eyes wide when he touched them.

She'd been told it was supposed to hurt, and it did a little bit. Like when she had her ears pierced. He didn't move much when he was inside her and it was very quick.

A dog was barking somewhere. Lost puppy.

When it was over and she pulled her knickers up, she realized her bottom was crusted with cool sand. The heat was over, along with summer. They walked the dunes in a flush of new shyness, talking of the beginning of their last year of high school.

Rose didn't tell anyone about it. She wondered if it showed. She looked at herself in the mirror and turned this way and then that way. She stood as close to the mirror as she could, leaning over the bathroom basin, looking into her own eyes until they disappeared behind the fog of her breath.

Looking for something. Some evidence that she was different.

Her mum had told her that she was a woman when her period started, but when her period started she was still playing with Barbies.

Surely now, though. Something had shifted inside her, a gear being ratcheted over a clunky cog, gaining torque, starting her up.

But it didn't show. How could all of these feelings not show?

At the dinner table Rose found herself staring at her distorted reflection on the back of a soup spoon, strangely pleased with the bulbous caricature smiling back at her. She was a woman now, but it didn't show and she couldn't tell anyone.

It always showed with Liv and Liv always told everyone. Liv was Rose's best friend and Rose was Liv's only friend. They were about as different as two people could be. Everyone thought it was odd that they hung around together — the good girl and the school bike.

Rose had asked Liv what being the school bike meant after hearing her called that by a girl who passed them in the corridor.

Liv laughed out loud before replying, "It means everyone's had a ride."

Their mothers had sat them next to each other on the first day of first grade. Liv used to say that their friendship had its seeds in nothing but geographical proximity, but Rose never forgot that first day of first grade when she peed her pants and Liv stood next to her holding her hand while all the other kids giggled and ran away. You stuck with the people who knew your humiliation history. At least, that's what Rose believed.

Liv started meddling with boys when she was twelve. That's what Rose's mum called it: meddling with boys.

"Don't meddle with boys, Rose," she would say, as if boys were an anthill and girls a sharp stick. Rose's mum wasn't a prude, but Rose distinctly remembered being told that girls had a "money box" and boys had a "whistle."

Rose learned most of the biological names for body parts from Liv. Liv was like a reconnaissance agent on the front lines. She went in, assessed the opposition, got felt up and reported back.

"It's called a fingeroo."

"I thought you said it was called a penis?"

Rose and Michael started dating almost by accident. They would go out with a group from school or church and find themselves standing together in queues or sitting together in movies.

It was when Rose started feeling self-conscious around Michael that she realized she liked him. That first awful time she had to turn and walk in the opposite direction from him in the school corridor and found herself pausing, ever so slightly, with the knowledge that her bottom looked like a stocking full of cottage cheese in those particular leggings.

Why, oh why, had she not worn a longer shirt? She had a class to get to, so she turned and walked away with her face inexplicably burning and one eyelid twitching. When she thought she'd given it enough time, she looked back and was mortified to find him still watching her.

But that's when she knew he liked her too.

Michael was the first boy Rose kissed properly. Really properly. She told Liv about that because she thought it was the most exciting thing she would ever do. Once they got it right. She was about to pike out on the whole thing when they finally sorted themselves and it started working the way it should. He tasted good and it wasn't too wet and he pulled her hair a little bit and she felt it in places far from her mouth.

She'd only been kissed by one other boy, and it wasn't like this. Jeremy Rislow kissed her at a party and it felt as if he needed to shave his tongue. Liv told her afterwards she'd seen Jeremy vomiting in the garden ten minutes prior. Then Liv had to hold Rose's hair back while she vomited.

Liv called Rose a late starter and told her she should have had sex by now. According to Liv, everyone else had had sex. And Liv had had sex with more than one boy.

"You're a bit of a late starter, Rosie. But don't worry about it."

"I don't. I don't want to have sex. Not yet."

"Okay. But take these anyway."

Condoms. A strip of condoms in shiny foil pouches that rustled guiltily in Rose's bag all the way home on the bus. They were still hidden behind a fat volume of nine-teenth-century poetry, bottom shelf of Rose's bookcase, when Michael slipped a finger inside her knickers on the beach.

She didn't even think of them. Until afterwards.

Rose wondered if she should tell Liv about it just to get her advice about the whole lack-of-a-condom thing. Liv was hard-headed, practical and strangely nonjudgmental for someone who was judged regularly and harshly herself.

But something gave Rose pause. She wanted to have this for herself and Michael alone, for a little while at least. She didn't want to take all those feelings that didn't show and dilute them by dissecting every moment of it until it was just a narrative of the mechanics for someone else's enjoyment.

Not even for Liv. Not yet.

2

Rose had been pretending to be someone else the day Michael decided he loved her. She was in the middle of dress rehearsal for the school play, standing on the stage in the school gym, her voice ricocheting off the polished boards with an intensity that set his bones ringing like a tuning fork.

He couldn't stop watching her. It wasn't that she was particularly beautiful, but there was an awkward loveliness about her gestures and intonation that set her apart from all the really pretty girls. She could hold Michael's attention simply because she wasn't seeking it.

In the middle of one of her lines, when she forgot the words, she filled her cheeks with air, squatted down on her haunches like a peasant in a paddy field, and twisted her hands together under her chin.

Michael started to laugh. Everyone started to laugh. Her costume was one of those old-fashioned full-skirted dresses like his grandmother used to wear, with a full bib apron over the top. He remembered her stockings and clunky brown lace-up shoes. And he remembered the line she got stuck on. He had no idea why it was so fresh in his mind. It might have been the way she said it, rising slowly up again with all that paddy-field vulnerability still in her face.

She seemed to look right at him and bawl, *"I want what I had before. You give it back to me. Give me back what you've taken."*

He didn't know why he should think of it now. It was the first thought he'd had all day other than when they might be able to have sex again.

He'd kept asking her, "Are you sure? Are you sure?"

His brother, Tim, had warned him about things like that. Having to make sure you have consent. How girls can sometimes say yes but mean no. Or say yes and then say no when it's over.

Tim also said to make his first time with a slut.

"It's like learning to drive in a rust bucket. Doesn't matter how many dents you put in it and then you'll know what to do when you're riding in something that's had a bit of spit and polish."

But Michael hadn't done it the first time with a slut. He'd done it the first time with Rose and he loved her.

He told his brother straight away. He walked into Tim's bedroom, shut the door and said, "I had … I did … you know."

"For Christ's sake, open the door!" was Tim's response.

They were not permitted closed doors. This rule applied to all doors in their house apart from their parents' bed-room door and the bathroom door, although there was a small battery-operated egg timer in the bathroom which their father said was to teach them to conserve water but which Tim insisted was to prevent wanking: "Have you *tried* to jerk off to that goddamn *tick, tick, tick, tick*? It's like fucking a suicide bomber!"

Michael opened the door and sat on the end of Tim's bed.

Even though he was fairly certain there was no one else in the house he whispered, "Did you hear what I said?"

"Yup. With that Liv girl, right? The school bike?"

"Rose."

"Oh. That's too bad."

"I … we … I didn't use a condom."

Tim put down his pen and turned to face Michael.

Tim was at university now, studying engineering. He was on the Right Path.

Michael had been hearing about the Right Path for as long as he could remember, and he believed in it. He wanted to walk that path too. He didn't have to find it first, or choose it from a delta of possibilities at a hazard-laden impasse. The directions were clearly marked.

Tim's advice was to make sure that, on any foray into the pleasures of the gutter at the side of the Right Path, Michael never take any substances that might interfere with stepping back up onto the path. And always, always use a condom.

Now Tim rested his pen lightly between his index and middle fingers and tapped the end against his desk, metronome-like, in a gesture Michael found disturbingly reminiscent of their father.

"But I gave you some."

Tim had given Michael a strip of condoms two years ago. Michael had seen their expiry date as a challenge. He would definitely have sex before they expired. But not with a slut.

He wanted it to be with someone he loved. Somehow that seemed less wrong. In the sixteenth century you could have sex with someone you promised to marry sometime in the future and the church said it was okay. Michael saw that in a movie once.

He loved Rose and wanted to marry her sometime in the future so that made it okay. His strip of condoms with their greasy innards and clearly stamped expiry dates were his pre-contract with Rose.

Except he didn't have one with him when they did it.

"I didn't have one with me when we did it," Michael said.

"You don't say."

"Will it be okay?"

"Are you asking me if your dick is going to drop off? Because it might be a good thing if it did, at least until you decide to use it responsibly."

Tim finally put down his pen. Michael realized he had been breathing shallowly in time with the *tick, tick, tick* of Tim's pen pulse.

"Look," Tim continued, "I assume it was her first time too, so you're not going to catch anything from something showroom new. So, yes, it'll be okay. Just don't do it again without one. Idiot."

And Michael knew there was real affection in that advice.

3

Rose felt mildly uncomfortable seeing Michael the following day. A subtle mixture of exhilaration and embarrassment made her pause when she saw him walking towards her.

Michael watched her approaching and saw her hesitation. Just a tiny tic at the corner of one eye betrayed her. She always got that when she was nervous. It was endearing.

Michael dithered for just a moment, as long as it took to accurately interpret her uncertainty, then strode towards her. With one hand clasped on the back of her neck he kissed her lightly on the cheek.

Without letting go, Michael whispered, "You okay?"

Rose nodded briskly.

Then she said, "You want to come over after school?"

"Yes." He knew then that it really was all okay.

Liv sidled up to Rose as soon as Michael had walked away.

"That was tender," she said, giving Rose's hair a tug. "Come on. Places to go, people to see, teachers to ignore."

The day crept on interminably. Each time Rose passed

Michael in the corridor they grazed hands. They would see each other's approach and position themselves such that one would drag their fingers across the back of the other's.

Somehow this small gesture had more significance than the usual body-slam hugging that had been their previous mid-hall greeting.

Previous. Prior to. Before. There was an intimacy to it that set a shallow bonfire alight in Rose's belly.

Last class of the day for Michael was physics. He was distracted and fidgety, a detail that wasn't lost on Ryan Littlemore, his partner in the current experiment.

They were supposed to be discussing the theoretical aspects of building and testing their own mangonel, but the conversation segued when Michael said, "Can a girl get pregnant if she's a virgin?"

"What, like the Virgin Mary? What the fuck do you think?" Ryan laughed.

"No, I mean if it's her first time?"

"You been poking Rose without a pro-phy-lac-tic?" Ryan broke the word down into deliberate staccato syllables, just loud enough to catch the interest of other students nearby.

"No," Michael said, returning to his diagram with vigor. "Stupid of me to ask someone who can't even find his dick to take a piss."

"Fuck off!"

"I've seen him take a piss." Sam Drake turned in his seat in front of them. "He can find it, Michael. It's just a very small threat." Then he dropped his voice to a whisper. "And a girl can get pregnant her first time. But it's super rare."

"No, they can't," Ryan said. "It's a myth designed to sell

morning-after pills. It's actually hard to knock someone up these days. Why do you think so many women are paying megabucks to get some doctor to fuck them with a turkey baster? Something to do with hormones in chickens."

"You're full of shit," Sam said.

"Boys!" Mr. Brooks intervened. "Are we on topic? Have you chosen your independent variable?"

"Hormones in chickens, sir?" Sam asked. The small group of boys sitting nearby caved in then to the laugh that had been simmering among them.

"Get on with it," Mr. Brooks said with a slight smile. Michael found himself drawing a chicken in his ballast bucket, determined never to bring the subject up again.

Rose was waiting for him in the carpark when class finished. They were going to go to her place. Rose's parents were never home until close to six.

Michael got off at the same bus stop as Rose and walked her home. He did this often. He called his mum from the bus and said he was going to Rose's for a bit and to expect him later. His mum said to make sure he said hello to Rose from her and would Rose like to come over later for dinner?

They stood next to each other beside Rose's bed. Michael had been in Rose's bedroom too many times to count, but this time it felt fascinatingly unfamiliar.

He was nervous. He hadn't been nervous on the beach. The full flush of urgency he'd felt in consummating their relationship on the beach had more to do with getting himself inside her before he lost it on her thigh.

He couldn't quite place the origin of his anxiety now, but he had a feeling it had something to do with wanting to get it right for Rose. Tim had talked to him about going down on a girl but Michael had never even seen one up close and was terrified he'd put his tongue in the wrong place. To him, kissing a girl between the legs was more intimate than going all the way.

Rose got into the bed, fully dressed. She began taking her clothes off under the covers. She didn't know why, but it seemed like the right thing to do. Michael touching things was different to him seeing things, and she didn't want him to change his mind. On the beach she hadn't even taken off her T-shirt or bra.

She had trouble getting her bra undone now, lying on her back with her arms buckled beneath her. Eventually she had to sit up, covers gripped under her arms so nothing showed, to unhook it.

She dropped all her clothes on the floor beside the bed except for her knickers. She noticed they were damp. She quickly wiped herself with them and then shoved them down the side of the bed that was against the wall.

Just as she realized the condoms were on the other side of the room in the bookcase, Michael took one out of his jeans pocket and put it on the bedside table. He took his clothes off in front of her, quickly, and then climbed into the bed.

They stayed in that position for a while, lying next to each other, necessarily squished together because the bed was a single.

Then Michael turned on his side. He looked at Rose's profile, watched her eyes scurry a bit under not-quite-closed lids, watched her lick her lips, watched the live flesh at the corner of her eye. He reached out and touched it, that jumping nerve that was so endearing.

Rose turned her face to him then and he began to trace a line down her face, her chin, her neck.

Then he pulled the covers down so he could see her. Rose found the embarrassment peculiarly exciting.

It was different this time. There wasn't the same resistance. He didn't have to push as hard to get inside her. He rested on his elbows so he could watch her face.

Her eyes were open. She was moving with him and he found himself making noises he'd never made before. Then Rose slipped her hand between their bodies and began touching herself.

Michael was stunned motionless when she did it. She closed her eyes and lifted herself against him to reconnect their bellies. It was an instinctual shove of her hips, but for just a moment Michael didn't recognize her. For less than a second, less time than it took for a synapse to fire, Rose had all the control.

When it was over they had to peel themselves apart like sheets of cling wrap. Michael turned to look at Rose's profile again. The twitch was gone and she was crying.

When he asked her if she was okay, she said, "I never thought I could be just myself with anyone."

Michael didn't know what she meant, but he lifted her hand and kissed her sweat-slicked palm.

Then she said, "Mum'll be home in a bit. You'd better get going."

Rose stayed in the bed after Michael had dressed and left. She didn't see him out because she didn't want to have to get up naked.

She knew she wasn't particularly attractive. She was the sum of a few good characteristics and she was reasonably content with this. Her mother had told her from a young age that she would never be a really pretty girl, but that she did have good child-bearing hips. Roomy, her mum called it.

So she stayed in bed and watched Michael dress. He wasn't shy of his nakedness the way Rose was. He was confident — tall and lean, with eyes as brown and flecked as her mother's tiger's-eye dress ring.

Before he left he leaned down and kissed her firmly on the mouth, pressing her lips into her teeth.

As soon as he was gone she rummaged for her secreted knickers and found they had dropped down under the bed. She noticed the sheet was wet under her and she could feel something dripping out of her.

That's when she noticed the condom was missing from the bedside table. Michael must have slipped it back into his pocket before he left.

Being a child whose privacy was well respected, Rose knew she didn't have to immediately worry about the sheets. Besides, she liked the smell.

She pulled her covers up, plumped her pillows and headed for the bathroom. She knew she had time to shower and dry the recess before her mum got home. She'd shower again after dinner so her mum didn't notice any change in routine.

Not that it really mattered. There was no way her mum was going to realize she had just had sex. Again.

Roomy girls didn't have sex in their bedrooms after school. Roomy girls married because they couldn't get sex in their bedrooms after school.

4

Rose's mother's name was Violet. It was an old-fashioned name and she had always felt self-conscious about it. When her only child was born she had decided to keep with the floral theme, and old-fashioned names seemed to be making a comeback, so she chose the name Rose. Her husband, whose idea it was to have a child, acquiesced.

Violet hadn't ever been sure she wanted children, but she had been told that the moment the midwife laid that slippery wrinkled infant on her chest she would fall in love. So she waited, for forty weeks, to fall in love.

When the moment arrived, she found that she actually fell in fear. Rose was the color of saffron, and her skin was dry and peeling and she seemed too fragile, for all her bawling strength. Violet stroked the fine down on her infant's ears and thought to herself, *This is how I started.*

And so she feared. No one knew, of course. Violet filled her eyes with tears and made the appropriate noises at the appropriate times, and everyone was pleased.

Violet's love grew as Rose herself grew. They were friends. They played together, ate together, bathed together and slept together. Rose's father was often away and even when he was at home he would give up his position in the marital bed to his daughter if Violet requested it. He thought their closeness charming and never felt excluded. He encouraged it, referring to his wife and daughter as "his girls." He only once approached his wife about the possibility of having another child. He came away disappointed.

Just hours after Michael left, Rose's family had a rare dinner together. Her father, Terry, was home for two weeks, soon to be gone for another six. He had lived this nomadic routine for so long that Rose considered him more a visitor than a father. He was a nice man who arrived unexpectedly — it always seemed unexpected even though the date was clearly marked on the calendar in the kitchen — with gifts and stories and hands that were cracked and webbed with dark lines of work grime.

He was telling a story now, his words whistling on his breath the way they did when he'd been without a cigarette for a few days. He wasn't allowed to smoke when he was at home.

"... and I swear that guy is solar powered. Something kicks in at sunrise. But after dark you can't get a word out of him!"

He laughed then, nodding and shaking his head like a balloon on a stick. His girls smiled and ate. A short silence ensued during which the smiling continued.

Then he said, "How 'bout I take my girls out to lunch tomorrow?"

"Rose has school, Terry. And I have work."

"So, you both play hooky for a day! Come on, it'll be fun."

"I have a play rehearsal after school too," Rose said quietly. Ordinarily Rose was the first one to support her father's slapdash ideas. But she wanted to see Michael tomorrow.

"Oh," her father said.

Rose registered his disappointment and felt slightly irritated.

He tried again.

"But you're the star, aren't you, Rose? Can't you be all artistic and moody and miss one rehearsal? Come on!" Terry leaned across and elbowed his daughter playfully.

"Terry," Violet said. There was a pause before she continued. "We can't just drop everything to entertain you. Rose has things to do. Important things. Maybe on the weekend we can all do something together."

"You said that last weekend," Terry responded.

"I'm sorry, Dad."

For just a moment, Rose felt the push-pull of being responsible for both of their feelings. It was a tiring ache that followed her about regularly.

"Don't apologize, Rose," Violet said. "You're not responsible for your father's feelings."

Rose heard the unsaid caveat: *You are responsible for mine.*

Violet wanted for Rose all of the things she felt she herself had missed out on. So she pushed Rose. Rose was smart, if not particularly attractive, and had talents, all sorts of talents. Violet was sure of it. It was just a matter of finding the right one.

So began years of ballet, calisthenics, gymnastics, drama, piano lessons — anything that captured Violet's imagination. Rose attended every lesson and event with mediocre success and unrelenting anxiety. Yet despite her clumsy foray into dance, for which her body was not built, and piano, for which her fingers were too short, a strange and welcome phenomenon occurred.

As Rose performed, Violet's fear lessened.

By the time Rose was a teenager, she was aware that maintaining the externals was absolutely vital to happiness. She understood, with an alacrity often observed in uncomforted children, that when you are sad there is nothing for it but to pretend otherwise. Rose had spent her lifetime watching her mother absorb arrows as if she not only refused to display negative emotion but was incapable of actually processing it.

Rose remembered a time when she had been bitten by a dog while riding her bike home from school.

As her mother tended the wound she looked up at her daughter's hot, wet face and said, "You're not crying, Rose. You're not crying."

Years later Rose realized this was far from a lack of compassion. It was her mother's way of coping with a frighteningly unpredictable world. And so Rose acted for her mother, the one aptitude discovered among a myriad of childhood activities. Rose realized she could easily pretend to be someone else. She was always in the school plays. She got used to walking around pretending to be someone else.

"Put on that happy face, darling," her mother would say. "A happy face reflects a happy home."

Walking the tightrope of happy-home dinner-table discomfort, however, seemed particularly tiring this evening.

As Rose charted the annoying silence that always followed Violet's parenting and Terry's sulking, she buoyed herself for the reparative save with, "Definitely this weekend, Dad. Right, Mum? We'll do something together."

"You could invite Michael," Violet said.

"Yes," Rose said.

"That'd be great, love," Terry said.

And Rose held her happy face right through the rest of dinner, her brain a snow globe with thoughts of the weight of Michael's torso sticking to hers.

She had never thought she could be just herself with anyone.

5

Liv was the place Rose first put her happy face down. Her safe place.

Liv was different from her other friends. She seemed to be able to see into Rose, deep down into her thoughts. Liv never judged. Liv just didn't care what people thought. In fact, Liv said life was just too damn short to bother trying to please other people, a concept Rose found both diabolical and unbelievably attractive.

Rose imagined the honesty she shared with Liv was how home should be. Liv and her mum sometimes yelled at each other and slammed doors and said fuck but then, always, squeezed each other tight with kisses and forgiveness. Rose had been in Liv's house and seen it.

Rose was spending the weekend with Liv. Rose loved Liv's house and she loved staying there. It was a house full of debris — always clean where it mattered but strewn with books and newspapers, elegant curios and chipped figurines, threadbare throw rugs and worn cushions, chess sets, dollhouses and pot plants.

It was the sort of mess Rose's mum wouldn't tolerate in

her own house but would describe as quaint and eccentric in someone else's — and then wash her hands vigorously when she got home.

Rose found the muddle comforting. Even though she visited regularly, she always knew that if she looked closely enough, if she wandered slowly enough, she would see something different. Some new bauble Liv's mum fancied from the op shop opposite the bus stop, or some long-forgotten treasure recovered from beneath something and given premium display space until it was eventually covered again.

Liv's bedroom was tiny. The other rooms of the house sort of spilled into it. There were old cups and saucers filled with jewelry, condiment jars crusted with wax from candle stubs, a stack of fusty-smelling board games and a rocking horse — no mane, eye missing — that had been rescued from a verge-side before it was carted off to a landfill.

There was no desk or study area. Liv lived on her big double bed. Her laptop lived on her pillow, the charger cord wrapped around one bedpost like a garland, snaking across the only windowsill and connected to a power point with suspicious burn marks on the loose faceplate. Rose often wondered if a mere jiggle of the plug would short out the entire house.

Liv and Rose had slept in that big double bed together since they were children. Rose liked it that way. She liked the weight and warmth of Liv next to her. It was like being in her mother's bed. In Liv's bed Rose felt comforted.

They sat cross-legged on the bed with two bags of corn chips, a jar of guacamole the consistency of Vaseline, and a plate of soggy microwave-heated party pies. Liv's mum's cooking was sparse and of dubious quality, so they filled up on the sort of stuff never imagined in Rose's kitchen. They'd probably have toasted sandwiches later.

"So." Liv dragged a finger across her lips and pushed a glob of dip onto her tongue. "Not seen much of you lately. Who have you been doing?"

It was Liv's standard opening to any conversation.

Rose hesitated and picked up a pie. She slowly peeled the pastry top off and began scraping out the stagnant layer of greasy meat-substitute with a corn chip.

She hesitated too long. Rose usually rattled off a list of the ugliest boys in school — as well as a couple of smarmy teachers — in response to this question, which inevitably ended with Liv butting in with "I've had that one!" and a descent into hysterical laughter.

Liv leaned across and gave Rose's hair a tug. It was something she had done to get Rose's attention since they were kids.

Rose had a weakness for contemplation comas. It had been labeled everything from ADD to plain laziness by the school. Liv didn't know what it was, exactly. All she knew was that when Rose was preoccupied with something big, she looked like a juggler on tippy-toes.

"What is it?" Liv said.

"Michael." Rose didn't know what she was going to say next. She hadn't even really been sure she was going to mention his name until she did.

"Oh no! You two haven't broken up, have you?"

"Michael and I — "

"Have broken up! Jesus — "

"Michael and I decided to — "

" — although of course, he is now free ..." Liv contin-ued, spitting a sharp shrapnel of corn chip back into the jar of dip. She laughed and snorted at the same time before saying, "Kidding, of course. I don't go out with anyone if there's no chance of a fuck, and as we well know Michael doesn't — "

"Have sex."

"Exactly," Liv countered.

"No! Are you listening to me? Michael and I decided to have sex!"

It was a blurt. Rose went hot and red with the exertion and relief of it.

Liv looked confused for a moment. Then she gave one of those back-of-the-throat laughs, a raw cadence of skepti-cism and, Rose thought, annoyance.

"Liar," Liv said.

Rose didn't respond.

"You're saying that to screw with me."

Rose felt the crook of her eye begin to tremble but still said nothing.

"Rosie?"

Rose proceeded to fill her now empty pastry shell with the sweet green Vaseline she so loved eating when she was there.

Then she took a bite and looked Liv straight in the eye.

That also confused Liv. Rose didn't look people straight in the eye. She remembered Rose telling her it was one of the things Michael's father didn't like about her when she first met his parents. Shyness could so often be mistaken for disdain. And this particular look in the eye was more than engagement, it was a demand. Rose had taken control of Liv's cynicism like a cat with its paw on a mouse's tail.

Liv noticed her shrapnel of chip floating in Rose's pie.

"Did you use a condom?"

"Yes. Well … no, not the first two times."

"Not the …"

Liv took a moment to gather in this information. She felt like she was herding butterflies in her head.

She swallowed and began again.

"Not the first two times. How many times have you done it?" she asked.

Liv never felt uncomfortable talking about sex. She and Rose talked about sex a lot. How much sex Liv was having, why Rose refused to have sex until she was married.

Liv couldn't understand her own uneasiness. It surprised and distracted her.

Rose was becoming uneasy herself. This was not the reaction she had expected from Liv. She had expected Liv to be jumping up and down on the bed by now.

"What's wrong, Livvie?" she asked. "I thought you'd be happy for me."

"I am. I am. How many times have you done it?"

"Ummm." Rose closed her eyes and smiled. "Lots."

"Lots." Liv knew she had to throw Rose a bone so she leaned forward and put her palms on Rose's knees.

She smiled and said, "I am happy for you. I am. So what was it like? Tell me *everything*."

Rose thought about it then, as she often did. She thought about the way it made her feel when Michael gently eased her legs apart with his knee. She thought about the way he looked at her, chin resting on her belly, knowing when he kissed her again she would be able to taste herself. She thought about his hand on the back of her neck, pulling her close to kiss her forehead. All the small unquantifiable details that meant nothing and everything.

What could she tell Liv? That Michael had put a vine around her heart and pulled it so tight that blood only reached her extremities when he was standing next to her?

Instead she said, "It's sort of private. And nice." Rose shook her head and giggled. "Not just nice. It's lovely. He's going to marry me one day."

"Oh, is he?" Liv jumped off the bed and left the room. She returned a few seconds later and threw a box of condoms into Rose's lap.

"They're from Mum's room. She lets me take them whenever I want. Now make sure you use them. Every time." She pulled Rose closer and planted a kiss on the top of her head. "Okay?"

"Okay," Rose replied.

Liv suggested they go to a movie. It wasn't unusual to go to the movies on a sleepover night, but Liv hoped she wasn't sounding too strident in her enthusiasm for the outing. She knew it would fill two hours with something other than continued conversation and she knew they could talk about the movie afterwards. That was at least four hours for Liv to perfect her best non-perturbed face and tone without the distraction of Rose crapping on about the loveliness of her fucking sex life.

Liv was jealous, and she hated herself for it.

6

Rose didn't immediately realize it, but she was watching the calendar. She was watching the calendar the way you watch a spider in the corner of a room you can't leave. Each day that passed was a spider leg twitching, a pedipalp shifting, and Rose went about her day with eyes relentlessly trained on that spider, so preoccupied with the passing time that ordinary considerations such as bathing and eating became ruthless irritations.

"For fuck's sake, Rose, are you going to wash your hair this week?" Liv had said, and Michael had asked her if she was feeling okay.

Initially she didn't think anything of it when she missed her period. The time came and went and although her lack of bleeding registered, she wasn't concerned. Sometimes she did skip a month. Sometimes it was so light she could get by with toilet paper alone.

Another month came and went, but still she didn't panic. Her breasts were tender, which always happened before her period started.

So she waited. There was some spotting in her knickers

one time, which excited her so much she washed her hair and shaved her legs, but she cried in the shower while she did so.

Eventually the spider began crawling up her arm. She knew she had to find out.

She used her student diary. She put dots on the pages where she had and where she should have. She added it up in her head and then she counted the individual days, touching each page of the diary with the ball of a pen so slick with ink that it skidded on some pages and left a small mark — amputated spider's legs pressed flat into the time that had passed.

Rose hated these gel ink pens. They were messy and sometimes the ball got stuck and important things became difficult to read. She could never go back over the patchy bits with gel ink pens either. They just left a wet mark that somehow always transferred to the heel of her hand.

When she had finished counting, she counted again.

Then she googled "My period is 61 days late."

Rose was relieved by the results. There were lots of people who were very late for all sorts of reasons. Stress and anxiety, sudden weight loss, recent illness, change in medication, change in routine. Rose had no idea her body was so fragile and unpredictable in its functioning. However, all the Google forums did advise a trip to the gynecologist to check things out. Just to be safe.

Rose didn't have a gynecologist. She had an ordinary doctor. The ordinary doctor was her mum's domain, though. Her mum took her to the ordinary doctor when she had tonsillitis, when she broke her finger playing softball, when she had the flu that turned out to be just a bad cold.

Rose didn't know if she could see the ordinary doctor without him telling her mum and dad. She didn't even have his phone number to make an appointment.

Rose started to text Liv, then put her phone down.

It was a short walk to the pharmacy. There were two near Rose's house, each in opposite directions. Rose set off for the one that was slightly farther away, the one rarely frequented by her mum. The one in the rundown shopping center with a carpark that was usually full of boys with lewd graphics on their T-shirts and skateboards under their arms that they slammed down in front of security guards powerless to enforce the No Skateboarding signage. It was these boys who prevented Rose's mother from patronizing this particular pharmacy, even though it was larger and better stocked.

Rose had to walk past a large protected swathe of bushland that bordered the main road in order to get there. This bush was famous for being the probable disposal site for a local woman who had been missing for three years.

Rose couldn't walk past without thinking about her. All the businesses in the area had had pictures of the woman up in their windows, including the pharmacy Rose was walking to now. Police in white jumpsuits had scoured that bushland for days on end, digging holes and shifting logs and eagerly trailing the skinny bottoms of wet-nosed cadaver dogs.

Still, the woman was never found. The police used the toilets in the petrol station across the road during that search, and Rose's mother drove out of her way to use a different one because of it.

The pharmacy was blasting its air con out onto the pavement so that crossing the threshold was like walking through a ghost. Rose browsed immediately near the door: deodorants, toothpaste, sanitary items. Moving forward and slightly to the left: vitamins, Band-Aids, denture adhesive, then a blood-pressure sleeve with an elderly man attached to it, struggling slightly as if he'd been detained by the equipment involuntarily.

Rose turned to cross to the other side of the shop floor and was intercepted by a middle-aged woman with bleeding lipstick and a name tag that read "Robyn."

"Can I help you with something, dear?"

"No. Thank you," Rose replied.

And that's when she saw them.

Pregnancy tests.

Behind the counter.

Rose had never really looked around a pharmacy before but for some reason she assumed that the only thing behind the counter would be prescription medicine. There were lots of things behind the counter that Rose knew you didn't need a prescription for: headache pills, cough medicine, condoms, nicotine gum, pregnancy tests.

Of course, she knew immediately why they were behind the counter. All the stuff most likely to be stolen by teenagers with either no money or too much shame was out of reach.

Robyn was still standing in front of Rose. Neither of them had moved. Rose had been prepared to buy a pregnancy test if she could have picked it from a shelf and presented it casually to a gum-smacking junior with bad manners. She had been prepared to steal one in the same circumstances.

But suddenly, being in this pharmacy with bleeding-lip Robyn guarding the altar of sacred goods made Rose short of breath.

So she said, "I just need a ChapStick."

Robyn immediately obliged by leading Rose to the point-of-sale items and presenting the options like a lip balm spokesmodel.

Rose grabbed one, paid for it and left, near to tears.

During the walk back home, past the lewd boys, past the bushland full of secrets — past the petrol station that still had a yellowing *Have you seen this woman?* poster, gummy with melting Blu-Tack, posted crookedly in the window — Rose realized there was only one person she could call.

The only person she could trust within her circle of friends was the friend on the outside of it.

She phoned Liv. "I need you to get me a pregnancy test."

Liv caught the bus to Rose's straight away. They decided to walk to the other pharmacy. It was closer and Rose couldn't go back to where she'd just come from. It would draw too much attention to her.

Liv walked into the pharmacy and straight up to the counter, past the people waiting for prescriptions, past the floorwalker who looked disturbingly like ChapStick Robyn, and asked for a pregnancy test.

Transaction complete, they walked home quickly. Despite the cool day, Rose could feel sweat-stench hardening on her body like varnish.

"I don't know how this could happen," she said.

"Let's see," Liv replied. "Did you share a toothbrush?"

Rose started to cry then. She felt the exact same fear she had felt when her piano teacher slapped her fingers with a ruler after she made a mistake. She felt the same humiliation she'd felt when her dance teacher told her she was shaped like a pear and needed to lose weight. And she heard the pitiless judgment in her mother's rant about Susan Johnson, the teen-tart who ruined her life last year by having a baby and dropping out of school.

Rose gripped Liv's hand and held it the rest of the way home.

7

When the little window on the little stick showed two bold pink lines, Rose was wiping wee off her hand on the hem of her T-shirt. There was some running down the inside of her thigh as well. She had gotten off the toilet too quickly, shaky and nauseous.

Liv had been on the other side of the bathroom door barking, "Mid flow, mid flow," like a coxswain.

When Rose finally emerged she gave the stick to Liv because Liv had her hand out for it. Liv marched back to Rose's bedroom then, so Rose followed.

It was not going the way she had planned. She had expected Liv to tell her that everything would be all right. She had imagined Liv would feel what she herself was feeling and not hate her for it. She had anticipated being comforted by Liv during those three minutes of waiting for the little window on the little stick to reveal its secret.

Instead Liv flopped onto Rose's bed and said, "Jesus Christ, Rose, it stinks of sex in here. Wash your fucking sheets."

And then those three minutes were gone and Rose's fear,

no longer a mere possibility secreted in her blood, curled up in her gut like a tapeworm.

"Are you going to tell Michael?" Liv asked.

"Of course."

"Why *of course*? You don't have to, you know. Ever thought that maybe you shouldn't?" Liv tugged Rose's hair.

"Why shouldn't I?" Rose asked. "Why wouldn't I?"

"Because you might not just be telling him. You don't know who he'll tell. You don't know who the people he tells will tell. Michael's a goddamn high-school superstar and if you ruin all that then I have a feeling you're the one who'll come out smelling like shit." Liv paused before adding, "He has a future, Rosie."

"So do I."

Rose had plans. They were her plans, hers alone, independent of those she'd heard her parents discussing on the rare occasions they were in the same place at the same time.

Her mother thought nursing was a good, sound career choice. Her father countered with something more corporate, such as advertising or commerce. Although Rose was present she had never been a part of these discussions. She was simply thrust at these possible futures in much the same manner she had been thrust at a gymnastics horse vault when she was eight. She had never been able to get herself over that thing.

But Rose wanted to go to drama school, a far too dangerously unpredictable future for her mother to cope with. So Rose kept her plans to herself, fearful that if given voice they would be denied as surely as her dog-bite tears.

Only Liv knew. And Michael. They had talked about

Rose auditioning and perhaps even winning a scholarship to attend drama school.

"I have plans too," Rose reiterated. "I have a future."

And Liv said, "Not anymore."

Rose told Michael the following day. She told him because she needed to. She needed someone to comfort her. Rose had expected that comfort from Liv, but had instead received a confusing combination of irritation and disappointment that seemed completely out of character for Liv.

So she told Michael and waited for what she needed.

He listened to her, like he always did, and managed during that first telling to hold her hand and keep the dread out of his face.

"What are we going to do?" she asked.

"Are you sure? I mean, can't you be wrong about this stuff? Make a mistake? Maybe we should get one of those tests from the chemist."

"I already have."

"Where'd you get that?"

"Liv got it," she said, and for just a second a flicker of distaste passed across his face. Not much, just a wrinkle of disapproval, which she saw and he felt. "You're worried about Liv knowing? I needed help!"

"I'm sorry," Michael said, but he let go of her hand and she burst into tears.

Michael had never understood Rose's attachment to Liv. Word around school was that Liv had had more dicks in her than a porta-potty at a construction site and was equally clean. He thought she was a slut and as influence always ran contrary to best intentions, he didn't approve of Rose's closeness with her. Ryan had more than once been lewdly suggestive about Rose simply because of her association with Liv.

For just a moment, with this new knowledge resting like a fistful of gravel in his throat, he wondered if Rose had been with anyone else. It was a brief guilty whisper in the one part of his head not deadened by shock and was immediately followed by the sick rush of panic.

He knew it was his.

"Have you told anyone else? Because I think — "

"No."

"Good."

They sat together on Rose's bed, not saying anything at all and not taking full breaths for a long time. Ever since Rose wee'd on that stick she felt like she hadn't taken a full breath. She felt like she would never take a full breath again.

Michael rested his elbows on his knees and dropped his chin to his chest. He could feel the pressure building in his eyeballs. His mouth gently filled with saliva and he let it pool at the back of his teeth.

When Rose's mum called out to him he couldn't answer at first.

"Michael, are you staying for dinner?"

Was he staying for dinner? He often stayed for dinner. Tonight it wasn't a good idea, though. He wasn't sure he could swallow.

"Um, no thanks. Not tonight." His voice sounded strange to him because he had replied through gritted teeth.

"You're not staying?" Rose grabbed his wrist and found herself gaping imploringly at his ear because he wouldn't turn to look at her.

"No."

"Are you angry with me?" She already knew the answer, and she felt herself growing angry in response.

He didn't say anything at first. He couldn't breathe, couldn't swallow, couldn't stay for dinner, couldn't speak.

She repeated the question. "Are you angry with me?"

"Yes," Michael said, and walked out of the room.

She didn't even hear the front door open and close. He was leaving quietly. He didn't want to draw attention to himself from her family, who liked and respected him and often let him stay for dinner.

In that moment she was terrified. She could have chased him down and pushed him into oncoming traffic. Wasn't that why animals attacked? Rose was sure she had read that somewhere, that animals attacked when they were frightened or threatened.

Yet Michael slunk out of there as if she herself was the threat.

"Rose, bring the towels in off the line and come set the table, please," her mum called from the kitchen. "Michael, you sure you don't want to stay?"

What should Rose tell Liv now? That she was right? That she shouldn't have told Michael anything at all? Did she really tell him because she needed to, because he had a right to know? Or did she tell him because it suddenly occurred to her that Liv might be right about their respective futures and if Rose really was going down, she had no intention of going down alone?

Rose brought the towels in off the line and set the table. The smell of whatever her mother had prepared was making her feel sick. All sorts of smells made her feel sick lately.

She took her place at the table and listened while her mum pottered and chattered, watched her mum dollop a mound of steaming vegetables onto each dinner plate, watched and prayed it wasn't fish she could smell, watched as a gray-looking fish fillet still awash in a slimy brown-butter pap was placed in front of her, watched it steam like wet rage, watched Michael getting angry, watched him not stay for fish and explanations, watched him leave, watched, watched, watched.

"God, Rosie! Terry, Rosie's sick!"

Watched her mum's mouth yelling the words to her dad who said things like "Oh, love," while helping her to her feet.

She wondered what all the fuss was about and then realized she had vomited. Her fillet was sopping with something altogether different now, and when she stood up, vomit dripped from her in semi-solid curds, pooling at her feet.

"She doesn't look well," said Mum.

"Time for bed, sweetheart," said Dad.

"Shower first, I think," said Mum.

"I'll clean up here," said Dad.

"Have you been feeling unwell, Rosie?" said Mum.

"Are you angry with me?" said Rose.

"Of course not," said Mum.

"Yes," said Michael.

8

Michael had always appreciated the fact that the walk between his place and Rose's was a short one. He could stay late at Rose's and be home in five minutes. She could stay late at his place and it only took him five minutes to walk her home. When it was raining, his dad would drive her home and that only took one minute.

For the first time he found himself wishing it was a longer walk. Five minutes was not enough time. Not enough time to set his face to its usual nonchalance, fix his voice to its usual casual pitch, and not enough time to snap his limbs out of the adrenaline rigor that threatened to choke his muscles and topple him into oncoming traffic.

That seemed odd to him too. Traffic still moving. People still going about their business. Everything and everyone performing normally, as if nothing had changed. As if the world were as it had always been.

Except it wasn't.

He had hoped that just this once he might make it to his bedroom undetected, if only to look at himself in the mirror and make sure nothing showed on his face.

But Tim caught him in the hallway as usual and in the usual way.

"Okay, what's the difference between a mosquito and a blonde?"

"Not interested," Michael said, pushing past his brother.

Ten steps to go. Nine. Eight steps. Seven. Six.

Close enough to reach out his hand and touch his bedroom door.

Five. Four.

"Boys! Dinner!"

Dinner was the big event in Michael's household. As Michael and Tim grew older and were home less and less, their father did insist that they make a concerted effort to be home for dinner. It was a testament to his parents' approval of Rose that an invitation to eat at Rose's was seen as an acceptable excuse to be absent from their own dinner table. Rose had even said grace at Michael's dinner table, a privilege usually reserved for family members.

But Rose wasn't there tonight. Michael sat at the table, his face cramping from the effort to maintain a smile, praying hard and fast that his father wouldn't make him say grace at the dinner table tonight.

When his father nominated Tim, Michael wondered if that was to be his very last answered prayer. It made him sad, and it made him wish he had prayed for something else.

"So," his dad said, hot on the tail of amen. "How are we? What we been doing? Who we been seeing?"

His dad had been using that line to open dinner-time conversation for as long as Michael could remember.

Michael was usually one of the first to jump in, but tonight he didn't think he could speak without something coming out of him that he couldn't control. Like tears. Like this dinner plate hurled across the room.

Tim always had a lot to say about how he was, what he'd been doing and who he'd been seeing. He was good, really good, thanks. He'd been studying hard but having to cut back on some extracurricular activities just to make sure he was on track for exams. He was seeing his mates regularly, playing squash and cricket on campus, organizing a student union protest against college fee hikes, and thinking of signing up for archery, just because it was something he had never tried and it might be a good way to unwind and What do you think, Dad?

Dad thought it was a great idea as long as it didn't interfere with Tim's responsibilities at home and at church. Had Tim forgotten he was supervising at the youth camp in the holidays and had three weeks of serving sacrament coming up?

No, Tim hadn't. Tim didn't forget his responsibilities. Or rather, when Tim forgot his responsibilities, he dodged detection.

"Michael?"

Everyone looking at him. Mouth full of food. Breathing through his nose. Michael suddenly felt raw. He was sure his skin had turned to tissue and every nerve ending twitched from exposure. This was a new and extraordinary sensation. Did it show? Had he dragged the smell of trouble back from Rose's bedroom? He could smell it. Could everyone else?

"Michael, I asked you how your day was," his dad said.

Squeak of knives on china. Everyone breathing, smell-ing.

"Good, yeah, good."

"You look tired, darling," his mother said.

And she said it smiling at him. The same smile she gave him first thing in the morning and when she put dinner in front of him at night and when he vacuumed for her.

She didn't know. It didn't show. None of them knew. He just looked tired.

"Am a bit."

"Just keep at it, son. These are the most important ex-ams of your life. Entry scores are everything these days, and medicine is competitive. And if there's anything we can do to help, you just let us know. You seem anxious. You've got to get a handle on that. Ask Timmo. He knows."

His dad said this, elbow on table, his knife waggling back and forth in the air like a metronome in six-eight. Michael nodded in time with the beat.

"Dad, it's only May. He's got months before exams," Tim said.

"Months that will fly," Dad replied quickly. "This is the year. The big year. Michael knows that."

"Michael's doing fine," his mum said.

It was a statement of fact. Michael's mum had always had the ability to bring things into being simply by stating them. Her reality didn't always correspond with everyone else's. However, her idealism had such an undemanding veracity that people had a tendency to just go along with whatever she believed. There was something childlike about her opti-mism. It brooked no resistance.

Michael's doing fine. He even believed it himself for just a moment.

"I'm not saying he isn't," his dad said, pausing to swallow and look around the table at each one of them. "He just doesn't want to let himself down."

Let himself down. He just doesn't want to let himself down. The words struck Michael in the torso like a fist. He was in a vacuum with his father's voice. Each paternal syllable rolled around inside him like the reflex to vomit.

"Impossible," Michael's mum said matter-of-factly.

Impossible. Caution converted to good cheer. It was impossible for Michael to let himself down. It was impossible for Michael to let anyone down. His mother had decreed it.

Again, for just a second, an involuntary bubble of fresh belief in his own promise pierced him. In that second he thought about telling them all about his A in today's maths test, beating his own record in the hundred-meter hurdles, being nominated as editor of the yearbook. He thought about asking Timmo to pass that potato gratin he loved so much and scraping all the baked cheese off the sides of the dish like he usually did. He thought about asking his dad to take him driving after dinner because he still had a bank of hours to work up for his logbook and he always enjoyed that one-on-one time with his dad.

He thought about all of this, all of the things he would do on any other night, for just a second.

But it wasn't a normal night and when he excused himself from the dinner table it was with a head full of things he might never say or do again.

9

We have to talk.

Rose had been sending the text all morning. Over and over.

Sent Items. Forward. Add Recipient. Michael.

And each time she sent it and received no response, she got angrier and angrier.

She liked the anger. It blocked out everything else. Rose had never felt this kind of anger. It was a squeeze-your-eyes-shut-to-stop-yourself-moaning kind of anger.

She had seen Michael today several times. They passed each other on the way to class, they stood in parallel canteen lines at lunchtime, they sat diagonally opposite each other at laptops in the library.

Rose had never seen him concentrate as hard as he did on that laptop. She couldn't even begin to imagine the discipline it took to refuse to look at her for a full forty minutes, and she took the snub like a bullet.

She sent the text again and watched him reflexively touch his pocket when his phone vibrated against him. And so her rage increased until she had to leave the library, afraid she might lean across and slam the computer screen down onto his fingers.

She wished she hadn't told him. Liv had been right. What had she imagined his reaction would be?

"Have you ever stopped to think he might be just as scared as you are right now, Rosie?" Liv asked.

"What?" Rose looked up, caught Liv's eye and looked down again. She knew she dropped her eyes too quickly, and she knew Liv would read into it.

They were sitting on the lawn cross-legged, facing one another, books in their laps. They were supposed to be studying. Mrs. Hensler thought it would be a good idea to sit out in the sunshine on such a beautiful day.

Rose would have been just as happy in a darkened room.

Liv leaned forward and tugged Rose's hair.

"You told him, right?" She didn't wait for a reply. "You told him and now he's acting like you loaned him money."

"What makes you think I told him?"

"The roses and engagement ring?" Liv whispered.

Their heads were so close together her breath moved a wisp of Rose's hair.

Rose moved away — just a smidgen, just a stiffening of the spine to increase the distance between them.

"Well, he's not sitting with you," Liv continued, "and he hasn't talked to you all day."

"He won't even look at me," Rose muttered. She was beginning to feel sick. She thought she might have been sitting in the sun for too long. Then she remembered.

"He *what*?" Liv asked.

"He won't look at me!" Rose spat.

Heads all around them popped up, startled meerkats sniffing the wind.

"Okay, settle down. *Everyone* is looking at you now."

Not everyone.

"What did you expect?"

"I don't know."

"Do you know what you're going to do yet?"

Rose studied her own lap. She felt vague and bewildered. Liv became tritely specific.

"Are you going to get an abortion?"

Rose looked up then. She heard the question from a long way away, as if she were eavesdropping on a bad phone line.

And she asked, "Do you think he still loves me?"

Liv had no choice but to be honest.

"I don't think anyone would put this much effort into avoiding you unless they loved you a great deal."

She had trouble saying it. A boy had never avoided her out of love, or intimidation, or pain of losing something well valued in the burn of proximity.

"Listen, Livvie, can you promise that you won't tell anyone? I mean, really promise?"

"Stupid question," Liv said. Then, "Do you know how pregnant you are? You know, how many weeks?"

"Not really. I mean, no."

"Well, don't you think you should find out?"

Rose felt confused for a second or two. She didn't want to know how pregnant she was. She didn't want things to get that real that fast.

All she could think about was Michael. If she could get him to look at her just once, she felt as if she could stop time, even send it spinning backwards, watch it unravel, come apart, spill away.

"Rose, you need to know how pregnant you are so you can think about … you know." Liv wasn't sure Rose knew at all. "You can't, you know … get rid of it if you're too far along."

Liv finished the sentence quickly, unsure if she had even been heard.

Rose knew that. She knew a time would come when it would take over all the hollows inside her and become a real thing.

But there was nowhere for her to go. No one she could go to who could stop time chewing at her raw edges. She felt faint with the fear of it.

Michael had to avoid her. The need to avoid her was as urgent and irrepressible as a sneeze.

He knew he couldn't do it forever. He knew it was unrealistic, unfair and infantile, but he did it just the same.

He even made sure that she was watching him when he read her text message and then shoved his phone back into his pocket with a force and finality that made her face cave in with fury. It gave him some relief to do so.

Ryan and Sam made the assumption that Michael had had a fight with Rose. They didn't ask many questions. They figured that if he wanted to talk, he would.

Ryan hoped he wouldn't want to. He thought Rose wasn't good enough for Michael anyway. She wasn't even that pretty. Even that slut bestie of hers was more attractive.

Sam made the obligatory derisive inquiry, referencing how honored they were that Michael would deign to spend a lunch break with them at all. But neither Ryan nor Sam pushed for information.

Michael didn't blame them. He didn't want to know personal stuff about them. Problems and fears and pain were off limits. Even a problem presented in the guise of irony was suspect in this group. The possibility of discomforting others kept them all focused on shared externals.

Sometimes they laughed about the well-publicized predicaments of people outside their own group. That one got caught shoplifting; she was on drugs; he brought a knife to school; that one's dad was in jail. But the talk was large and hearty — jovial, cautionary tales to make them feel better about their own small stuff. Their own unshared stuff.

To bring any such crisis into their inner circle would be seen as a betrayal. Michael was sure he would not be forgiven for it. And what's more, his predicament would probably become one of those well-publicized cautionary tales by the end of the day.

He wondered if Rose had told her mum. He supposed not. Surely her mum would go straight to his mum.

What then? His dad. Tim. Friends at church and friends at school. Shock and disappointment and anger and change. Everything changing. The future changing irrevocably in an instant.

No, not in an instant. Perhaps instantaneous change would be easier to deal with. This would be a change that skulked and shimmied over a long time, torturous and unpredictable as evolution. Life would become volatile and random, change stacked upon change over weeks, months, years.

Could they get rid of it? Michael knew people did that all the time, but he had no idea how they went about it. She'd have to go to a doctor.

Was that kind of thing confidential? She was only seventeen. Would the doctor have to tell her mum (his mum, his dad, Tim, friends at church and friends at school)?

Did you have to pay for it? Michael had some money. He knew Rose had some money too.

Did you have to stay in hospital for something like that? How would they explain that to her parents? She couldn't go to hospital without them knowing.

Maybe you could get it done in a chair, like getting your wisdom teeth out. Michael had had his wisdom teeth out in a chair and that was major surgery. They might be able to pull it off if it could be done in a chair.

How hard could it be? This tiny thing, just a lump of cells, a clot, a smudge of tissue deep up inside her, unstable and vulnerable. Surely removing it couldn't be more complicated than picking your nose.

He had to talk to her. They had to get this thing settled.

Meet after school in skate park. Need to talk.

10

Rose got to the park before him. Michael saw her sitting on the picnic table waiting as he approached. It made him uncomfortable, this watching of his approach. He became conscious of his gait, the set of his shoulders, the heat in his chest.

And he became conscious of her. For the first time since all of this began, he became conscious of her.

He cared about her. He had forgotten that.

"You bastard!"

He didn't see it coming. Rose launched herself off the table and swung. She had never hit anyone in her life, so it was a paltry attack. Michael ducked, but not before Rose managed to dig her fingernails into his scalp. She pulled away hard, her hand cobwebbed with a lattice of Michael's hair.

"Are you fucking mad?" Michael hissed, staggering backwards. He meant to scream it but his breath was gone.

"No! You are! Remember? Mad at me? Angry at me? Remember?"

Rose lurched back and forth in front of him, tottering on the balls of her feet, standing her ground while wanting to run.

She had more to say, she had rehearsed it all, but now the

moment was here all she could do was stand there, pitching like a dinghy in the wind, making a strange mewling sound to stop herself from crying.

Michael took a step forward. Then another. Then he sat on the bench, rested his elbows on the table and slowly placed his head in his hands.

Without looking up, he said, "Remember the play?"

When Rose didn't answer he continued, "I just thought of *Seventeenth Doll* and how good you were in it. I never liked plays before I saw you in that one. Thought they were stupid. Boring. They mostly are. But not that one."

"You came to every performance."

"Yeah," Michael said. "I did." He slowly dragged his face through his hands then, catching his bottom lip with his fingertips, revealing the thick pink flesh on the inside.

Rose sat heavily opposite him and stretched her hands across the table between them. Michael dropped his hands on top of hers.

"Are you all right?" she asked.

"No."

"I mean, are you *all right*?" Rose said, pointing gingerly towards Michael's head.

"Oh, yeah." Michael pulled strands of his own hair from between Rose's fingers.

"I'm sorry," he said.

"Me too."

He looked at her then. He hadn't noticed how pale she was. Like she had the flu, or hadn't been sleeping.

Rose turned her hands over so that their palms were touching.

"I was good in that play, wasn't I?"

"Hmmm."

Rose asked again. "I was good, wasn't I? Michael, do you think I'm a good actor?"

"Yes, Rosie, you're a really good actor."

Rose squeezed Michael's hands before saying, "How good are you?"

Rose remembered *Summer of the Seventeenth Doll* too. On opening night she had a virus, or food poisoning, or something that made her weak and nauseous and sweaty, but she didn't tell anyone. She had to be sick in the toilets twice before she went on stage and once when she was in the wings. She had to vomit into a towel that time. Liv got rid of it for her. Rose had no idea where that towel ended up, but she never saw it again.

And it was all because of Louise Wright. Louise believed, with a vehemence that convinced complete strangers, that she was going to be the next Nicole Kidman. In fact, she acted as if she already was. The shock of not being cast in the play that year kept her home from school for a week. Her mother even complained to the principal, the consequence of which was Louise being cast as Rose's understudy in the role of Olive. She would come to cast rehearsals dressed for a red carpet and overact all over the place, like a dog marking its territory. She argued with the director, criticized her fellow actors mercilessly and displayed an uncomfortable level of delight when Rose got a cold sore a week before curtain.

Louise Wright managed to demonstrate exactly why no one wanted to work with her.

Ergo, when Rose got sick on opening night, she hid it.

And she hid it well. There was no way she was going to allow Louise Wright to step in. Apart from the fact that Rose hated her, she knew she'd need a shoehorn to get Louise back out of the role for the rest of the run.

Rose felt terrible that whole night. But apart from Liv, no one knew. It was simply a matter of wanting to play the part more than wanting to give in to the virus.

Rose was learning about viruses in biology. *Virus: a submicroscopic particle of a nucleic acid surrounded by protein that can only replicate within a host cell.* They only functioned inside the cells of another living thing. A virus was a parasite. Viruses were not considered to be independent living things. And they could be flushed out.

"We should tell someone."

Even as Michael said it, he wasn't sure he believed it. Telling someone else, anyone else, would be an extension of the shame, and he was stretched to capacity as it was.

His parents had always been there for him. They loved him. He didn't doubt that.

But wasn't love based on belief? And wasn't belief just expectations all dressed up for opening night?

This was his last year of school. The opening night of the rest of his life was only months away. His mum and dad had bought and paid for their expectations.

What happened when someone lost that? What happened when someone stopped believing in you? And even if his father could get past the initial shock and regret, wouldn't it still be there, that germ of disillusionment, feeding on the insides of his love for Michael, just as much a virus as this thing inside of Rose?

Michael knew his father had been raised by a man who slowly drank himself to death for no other reason than he had a real taste for it. His mother told him about the grandparents he had never met and why. She told him how often Harold would find his stepfather sitting at the kitchen table, loved-up and urine-soaked, wanting to talk, or alternatively screaming and throwing things, occasionally slapping his mother.

Harold didn't want that for his own family. He decided the only way to survive the volatility of the world was to take the guesswork out of the equation by way of God's law and household rules.

Harold's rules were simple and indisputable. He expected his sons to do as they were told. Harold lived by 1 Timothy 3:4. He was one that ruleth well his own house, having his children in subjection with all gravity — and he called this love. He guided his family along an undeviating path of interaction with the world without worldliness.

If his choices for his sons sometimes seemed harsh, or unforgiving of the natural circuitousness of childhood, it was not as a result of a lack of genuine care. It was simply that he did not trust the world or the people in it. He wanted to create something worthwhile and lasting for his two boys.

"You have to remember, Michael," his mother had said. "In a world of storms you build shelters. You do not sit on the beach watching the clouds roll in. That's how your father sees it. He is not an unkind man, so please do as he asks."

Sometimes Michael wondered if he might be selling his

father short. But when he looked at Rose sitting opposite him, her fingers curling in towards his wrists, he knew this wasn't the time to test the extent of his father's charity.

"I don't think we should tell anyone," Rose said.

"Me neither."

"But you just said — "

"I just thought I should say that in case it was the right thing to say," Michael said.

"Well, can you just say what you really feel from now on?" Rose tried to curb her impatience. She continued quickly, the words blurted out as if racing a paralysis that would shut her up forever. "I've worked it out. We don't tell anyone. No one could help us anyway. I can hide it. It's not real."

Rose said it again inside her head, a counterpoint to the words coming out of her mouth. *It's not real, it's not real, it's not real.*

"Anything could happen. We could tell people and then it could just go away and everything would be ruined for nothing!"

It could just go away, it could just go away, it could just go away.

"These things go away all the time. You have to promise me you won't tell anyone."

Rose realized she was gripping Michael's wrists so hard her knuckles were white. She could feel his pulse, much slower than her own.

She hated that his heartbeat didn't betray him. Was he even listening?

"Michael! You have to promise me you won't tell any-one!"

"Okay," Michael said. He slowly pulled his wrists away from Rose. "What now?" he asked.

"Nothing now." Rose stood up. She suddenly realized she was exhausted. Her bones ached. "I'm so tired my hair hurts," she added before walking away.

11

Rose could smell everything. The open box of bicarb her mum shoved in the back of the fridge wasn't working. Every time Rose opened the door a tinny wave of asparagus stench wafted out, and she was pretty sure there was an old banana in there somewhere. The lavender fabric softener her mum used sat in the back of her throat all day and made it hard to eat. The school gardener had spread fresh mulch. The combined tang of woodchips and zoo poo made her gag.

The smell thing was affecting her mood too. It wasn't the smells alone that bothered her. It was also the anticipation of coming across a smell that would set her off. Her dad's ginger tea, brewed morning and night and usually a welcome and comforting aroma, made her scream shut up at him when he asked her if she was feeling unwell.

Rose couldn't understand the smell thing. It was like a superpower. It changed everything about her for seconds at a time. She would forget where she was and what she was doing in the grip of olfactory assault.

Rose googled "miscarriage" and found out it was also

called spontaneous abortion. She found the term reassur-
ing.

All sorts of things caused spontaneous abortion. It happened a lot too.

The more Rose read, the more amazed she was that anyone actually carried to term. Sometimes the thing developed wrong and was rejected by the body, just pushed out
as if it had never been there. Sometimes a bad shock or in-
jury made it go away.

Rose had been in a state of shock since she first discovered it, so maybe it was already gone.

Just in case this thing was stronger than her own distress,
Rose took the precaution of following one online warning
very carefully. She discovered that some anti-inflammatory
drugs could cause spontaneous abortion. Her fingers shook
and she couldn't focus for tears as she popped aspirin and
ibuprofen out of their childproof blisters, swallowing hand-
fuls of the bitter-tasting generic substitutes that her mother
bought for budgeting reasons.

Then she hastily deleted her browsing history.

Liv told Rose that the smell thing was a symptom of
pregnancy. Rose told her it couldn't be, because she wasn't
pregnant anymore. Rose was beginning to find Liv clingy
and overinvested. She told Liv to go and make some other
friends. She told Liv to get herself a boyfriend.

Liv's mother had a saying: No good deed goes unpunished.
She was a woman never surprised by ingratitude, discourtesy
or the unpredictable behavior of the human species. With
such low expectations of the world, Liv's mother was a woman
very rarely disappointed and very often highly amused.

She was chuckling now.

"So Rosie is knocked-up and now she wants nothing to do with you," she said.

"Well, she says she's not pregnant anymore."

"But you're still on the outer?"

"Yeah."

"You tried to help her, didn't you?"

"Not really," Liv said.

She suddenly felt the need to examine and justify every interaction of the past few weeks. She had a feeling she hadn't helped enough.

"Well, I just listened to her, you know?" Liv wondered if she really had listened. "I bought the test for her. I just mainly sort of ... listened."

"Just mainly sort of, huh?"

"She hasn't given me a reason for treating me like shit or anything, Mum. She said I should get other friends, get myself a boyfriend or something."

"A boyfriend, huh? Because the boyfriend thing worked out so well for her."

"I don't know what to do."

Liv had never been without Rose. When Liv saw Rose now she felt a bit choked. No one had ever told her that grief was like trying to swallow a fat watermelon whole and she had a feeling she had picked out the watermelon all by herself by not holding Rose's hand this time when she peed herself.

What bothered Liv even more was Rose seemed to be enjoying this withdrawal from the friendship. She seemed extremely happy.

"Stay out of it," her mum said.

"Should I tell someone?"

"Tell someone what? You said she wasn't pregnant anymore."

"Can that happen?" Liv asked. "I mean … does it happen often?"

"Not often enough," her mum said with a quiet laugh. "Look, I don't know what's going on with Rose. Maybe she is and maybe she isn't. Doesn't matter. You know something about her that she doesn't want to be true. Every time she sees you, even if you never speak of it, she'll hear what frightens her most clanging like a bloody bell."

"That's stupid."

"That's people. Stay out of it."

Stay out of it. Stay out of it. Stay out of it.

Liv said it to herself over and over and then over again, waiting for some internal verification, that click of instruction shifting over to common sense. She thought she might be able to coach herself into believing it if she said it often enough. Friendships ended all the time for all sorts of reasons. Sometimes they ended for no reason at all. This one had an ending that was hogtied to a beginning, a beginning Liv knew about.

When Liv passed Rose at school, Rose laughed too loud. She gripped Michael too flamboyantly. She linked arms with other girls too ferociously. Every exaggerated joy Rose staged and performed for Liv felt like a drive-by shooting.

Liv began to get angry. She was paying a high price for unwanted knowledge.

Liv was in the toilets when she heard them talking about her. She was accustomed to hearing other girls talk about her in the toilets and would usually wander from her cubicle and nonchalantly present herself to the jury of her peers with a well-chosen digital gesture and a smart mouth.

But this time Liv heard a voice among the others that stopped her cold.

Rose.

"You're well rid of her. I mean really, Rose. What'd you two fight about anyway?"

It was Tiffany Cross, otherwise known as Blonde Ambition and often referred to by teachers as a "good example."

"Nothing really," said Rose. "We just grew apart." Her vowels distorted in a way Liv recognized immediately: Rose applying lip gloss. "And we're not kids anymore, you know? She's not going anywhere. She's got no plans for the future."

"And she's a slut." Holly Darrow, who Liv knew for a fact offered blowjobs at parties after a few vodka cruisers. But these girls didn't consider blowjobs to be sex.

From the laughter that followed, Liv guessed there were about five of them. She recognized Rose's laugh. Studied the pulse of it for any sign of coercion, anything to suggest Rose wasn't really joining in. But she was.

Liv wanted to step out from behind the door, slap Rose's face, ask Holly about the calluses on her knees. But she couldn't.

"That's harsh, Holly." Liv had to squeeze her eyes shut when she heard Tiffany patronizingly defend her. "Liv is just … limited. Right, Rose?"

"All I know is that I have to think about my future," Rose

said. "And be with my real friends now. I'm not going to be around next year anyway. I'm going to study acting and do something with my life. Liv just drags me down. I can't stand it anymore."

"Like I said, Rosie, well rid of her."

The last thing Liv heard over the washing of hands and brushing of hair was enthusiastic questioning of Rose about which drama schools she was going to audition for.

Liv waited in those toilets for three hours. She skipped all her classes, waiting in the toilets knowing that Rose would eventually have to pee. She knew these were the toilets Rose went into, the same toilets every time even if her classes were on the other side of the campus. She even knew which cubicle Rose used.

So Liv waited.

When Rose finally walked in, Liv was sitting on the toilet floor next to a row of basins.

Rose had never seen Liv looking like this. Liv was picking nail polish off her toenails, one leg tucked right up to her shoulder, the other crooked towards her.

Liv unfolded herself quickly and stood up looking angry, her face a tight whitewash. Rose considered turning around and walking out again, but the situation was a test. If she could continue to withhold, if she could breathe through the missing of Liv just as she did a sickening waft of ginger tea, without revealing anything, then the play would continue.

Rose set her face.

"Why are you doing this to me?"

Liv hadn't meant to start this way. She had rehearsed an

approach that was reasonable and non-confrontational. She had imagined a re-ignition of their alliance based on eye contact alone.

She was, however, completely unprepared for Rose's cold stare and small smile. The sort of smile you give someone you don't know and accidentally get too close to on a crowded bus.

There would be no copacetic crumbling of barriers.

"I don't know what you mean," Rose said, brushing past Liv to get into the toilet cubicle.

"Yes, you do."

Liv suddenly found herself staring indignantly at, and speaking desperately to, a closed toilet door.

Panic set in. Just a little bit, but enough to set a trill in her stomach and make her swallow hard.

"Why are you ignoring me?" Liv continued. "I haven't told anyone anything. I'm not going to tell anyone anything. What did I do to you? Tell me what I did to you!"

"I don't know what you're talking about," Rose said from behind the door.

"Yes, you do!" Liv said, kicking the door. "This is bullshit! Talk to me!"

Liv was on the verge of tears. She swung her leg forward to kick the door again just as Rose unlocked it. The door flew inwards, rebounding hard against the inner wall of the cubicle. A rush of air slammed Rose in the chest as she caught the door in her hand.

In that moment, the shock of almost being hit by the door stripped Rose's face. Liv saw it. For just a second Rose's eyes were recognizable.

But it didn't last. The vulnerability Liv saw in Rose's eyes was shut down with a resolve that was palpable.

Rose pushed past Liv and walked out. She was deleting her browsing history, and Liv was a part of that.

Liv sat on the floor of the toilets until the lunch bell sounded. Then she got up and went home.

12

Michael had never thought much about time, because he had always believed he had all the time in the world. But he was beginning to think about it now. In physics they learned about Einstein's theory of relativity, a theory that Michael clung to with increasing desperation as another season clicked into place without word or warning. There was no gentle shift from mild to cold days. Winter fell in on the year like a kick in the heart, changing everything and nothing.

If time wasn't real, if it were truly relative to the position of the observer of its passing, then why did it feel as if the air was being squeezed from the small vestibule of time Michael and Rose had left?

There were only five months left until exams.

There were only five months left until.

When Michael tried to talk to Rose about it she simply said, "Five months left until what?"

It didn't help that preparation had become the raison d'être of the scheduled school day either, heightening Michael's already hair-trigger sensitivity to the fact that he and

Rose had other things they needed to prepare for. There was unscheduled testing, mock exam papers, discussion of study procedures and relaxation techniques. Career advisers and guidance counselors worked their way through the student body with group meetings and individual appointments to ascertain who should be removed from the roll prior to commencement of exams. Those who weren't going to pass were given alternative paths for their own good and the good of the school. No need to pull down the campus average by allowing no-hopers to screw up the curve.

At least, that's how Tim described it.

"They'll clear out the plebs," he said at dinner one night.

"Oh Tim," his mother countered. "I'm sure that's not true. I'm sure everyone is given an equal chance to succeed."

"Nothing wrong with getting shot of the hoi polloi," Harold said. "Natural selection, right, Michael?"

"What?"

"The fact is, weeding out occurs throughout life. You only get a certain number of chances. You don't waste them." Metronome knife. Swig of water.

"Yes, I'm sure you're right," his mum said.

"What about mistakes?"

Michael didn't understand why he was suddenly angry with his dad. He loved his dad, respected him, feared him. His dad had been his divinity since he was a little boy. He could remember sitting in church fingering the buttons on his dad's suit jacket, pinching mints from the stash in his dad's pocket, believing God smelled just the way his dad did, and that God probably had the same jacket buttons and deep pockets. It gave him great comfort to give God his father's face, and even when he came to the understanding that it wasn't his own father tapping into and answering his silent prayers at night, he was still grateful for that early childhood misconception.

It had never occurred to him that his father could be wrong about anything. Even now the possibility made Michael extremely uncomfortable.

"Mistakes? Don't make 'em!"

Tim said it with a mouthful of food and then laughed just hard enough to spit a piece of ham steak back onto his plate.

"Michael asks a good question and it's nice to hear from him," his dad said, making reference to Michael's consistent and increasingly doleful silence at family meals.

When his dad didn't continue, Michael said it again. "What about mistakes, Dad?"

"What do you think about mistakes, Michael?"

This was one of his dad's favorite maneuvers. He would take a question and redirect it at the inquirer so that they were obliged to respond in a way that pleased him. Michael had always thought of it as shrewd and instructive. Tonight he saw it as dexterous and controlling.

Realization of his own judgment about the move distressed him more than his father's use of the strategy.

So he simply said, "I don't know, Dad. I suppose I'm not very well equipped to deal with mistakes."

"Then I've failed you," his dad responded, carefully placing his knife and fork onto his plate and tenting his fingers beneath his chin. "This disappoints me."

A strained silence ensued. Michael knew what his father

required, and that in itself made him angrier. His father wanted reassurance.

Tim breathed slowly and loudly through his nose, warranting a sideways glance from Dad. His mother stopped eating.

"You haven't failed me," Michael acquiesced.

His father immediately picked up his cutlery.

His mother resumed eating.

"I didn't believe so, but I would want you to be honest," his dad said. "As for what I think ..." And here he paused to chew and swallow and clear his throat and place his knife and fork side by side on his plate as he always did when he was going to use his hands to speak. The chink of stainless steel on china rang like a bell. "I think there are degrees of error and that error has to be disciplined. These students being winnowed out before exams are reaping what they sowed. They either didn't work hard enough or have not shown the requisite commitment to deserve further help."

"Amen," said Tim.

"I'm not finished yet!" his dad snapped. But it seemed he had lost his train of thought because he did finish then, with this: "Degrees of error, Michael. Opportunity is fragile."

They continued to eat. Even though Michael ate quickly, he found himself having to heave his senses through the slowly passing minutes, dragging his consciousness after him like a dying dog.

He thought about those last words his father had spoken. *Opportunity is fragile.* He had been hearing the same sentiment expressed at school lately, although obviously intoned with far more optimism and enthusiasm. It was funny how the same aphorism could be peddled as either hope or admonition.

Of course, the school guidance counselor didn't use that exact phrase, but the implication was the same. Two sides of the same coin. Michael's future was a fragile opportunity that he should be both grateful for and terrified of.

There hadn't been much for Michael to discuss with the guidance counselor when he had his appointment earlier in the day. Michael wondered how this woman decided to become a guidance counselor.

Had she herself sat in his chair one afternoon, years ago, and said to the person sitting opposite, "I want to do what you're doing now"?

If she had, and if she'd ever had any sort of passion for the position, that time had long since passed. She seemed inappropriately poker-faced for someone who was supposed to be inspiring others in their chosen career paths. She sighed a lot and kept scratching her armpit.

"Good grades, good subjects, good attendance record, good reports." Sigh. "You can pretty much do anything you want. You're very lucky to have such opportunities ahead." Said in a tone that implied choice was a bad thing. Sigh. "So, what do you want to do?"

"I'm going into medicine," Michael had replied.

Sigh.

This is the woman students come to with their personal problems, Michael thought. Problems with teachers, problems at home, problems with friends. There was even a boy in a wheelchair who used this woman's office when he had to pee. Everyone knew about that.

Michael couldn't smell pee. There was a door leading to another office, an inner office behind the guidance counselor's desk. Maybe the wheelchair boy peed in there. Maybe the people with real problems went in there and there was someone else, someone who didn't sigh and scratch, someone who listened to problems all day long, someone only certain people had access to. The very deserving, the very disturbed, the very disabled.

An inner sanctum. The holy of holies.

Michael imagined what it would be like to just say it. As the words formed in his head he could already feel the relief of it, the unburdening, the respite from responsibility, all the proper grown-ups stepping in with options for his now terribly fragile future. *My girlfriend is pregnant and doesn't want me to tell anyone and I don't know if that's the right thing or not and I'm scared and stupidly angry at her when it's not just her fault and now I've let everyone down and nothing I do from now on will mean anything because of this one mistake.*

But he didn't say it. There was something blatantly uninviting about this scratching, sighing woman in front of him.

"Well, here is some information on the different campuses and their criteria. Application forms, subject handbooks, contact numbers. Feel free to make another appointment if you need anything else. You can make appointments through the registrar. Good luck with your preparation."

13

Rose knew her mother was suspicious. For a start, she'd hidden the ibuprofen.

Violet was almost certain Rose had a virus. She wanted to take Rose to the doctor and find out why she was so tired and why she didn't feel like eating.

The truth was, Rose *did* feel like eating. She was hungry all the time, and the crawling pain that hollowed her out when she denied herself food became addictive and satisfying. She began denying herself more and more, with the zeal of a flagellant. She marveled that she could manage to lose weight rather than gain it. The tiny swelling below her bellybutton was hardly noticeable.

Rose even allowed her mother to see her naked, such was her faith in her control over her own body. She knew it would be more suspicious to refuse her mother access to the bathroom while she dried off after a shower. They often used the bathroom at the same time and Rose had discovered that people very rarely saw what they were not looking for.

Her mother merely commented that Rose was looking pale and a bit drawn. Rose felt like laughing, so she did. And her mother laughed too and it was as it always had been. Rose felt powerful and happier than she had in weeks.

Violet tried cooking only Rose's favorite foods. She kept bowls of fresh fruit out and convinced herself that Rose was probably grazing between meals. She bought multivitamins that the chemist told her were specifically formulated for teens and placed one on the breakfast table every morning next to Rose's cup of tea. It always vanished and Violet convinced herself that Rose was swallowing it.

She noticed that Rose's weight loss seemed to be accompanied by a kind of emotional shrillness Rose had never displayed before. Rose was high-pitched happy, her movements and responses as sharp as her collarbones. Violet put all this down to the stress of final exam preparation and the fight that had suddenly ended the lifelong friendship between her daughter and Liv.

Rose's mother did, however, check under Rose's bed and in Rose's wardrobe for jars of vomit. She had seen a midday movie once where a girl with an eating disorder purged into jars and stashed them in her bedroom.

Violet didn't find any vomit and was so relieved she stopped looking for anything else. People rarely saw what they were not looking for.

Sometimes when Rose thought she was unobserved, her mother could see a tiredness there that seemed more than physical. She would always ask, "Rose, are you all right?" And Rose would smile and say yes and her mother would accept this because her love and her worry were already webbed with greenstick fractures and she didn't think she could cope with honesty. Not just now. Not yet.

And besides, it was none of her business.

Rose started smoking when she found out it starved the placenta. She found out it starved the placenta in biology. She rarely paid attention these days, so she was pleasantly surprised when her brain was able to filter out this one piece of applicable information. Smoking restricted blood vessels thereby reducing the flow of oxygenated blood through the placenta. The placenta was starved. The fetus didn't grow properly.

Rose heard "carbon monoxide" and "cyanide" and "starving" and "stillbirth."

Starving. She already knew girls at school who smoked to reduce their appetite, but it suddenly had further-reaching implications for Rose. Smoking could keep her weight down, as well as possibly get rid of this virus inside her. Pollution, after all, had been known to close down entire cities for days.

She imagined her internal organs being wrung like a tea towel, blood flow restricted, arteries atrophied, bones clunking together as her skin wrapped around them like parchment. The virus starving.

It was easy to pinch cigarettes from the packets her father bought to take back to work with him. When she first started smoking it made her sick and she was relieved to feel this different kind of sickness. She had to go to bed as soon as she got home from school because she felt like she might vomit. Her chest burned, and her mouth tasted like a shoe smelled.

She wasn't brave enough to use the smokers' toilet at school. Everyone knew about the smokers' toilet. Even the

teachers, who regularly raided it. They rarely apprehend-
ed anyone. No one finished a full cigarette in there. It was
a place of quick drags, frenzied flushing and back-slap-
ping congratulations at triumph over the system. It always
smelled bad and there were usually a few floating butts in
bowls.

Everyone knew the girls who used the smokers' toilet.
That's why Rose avoided it. Being seen by a regular in those
particular toilets would be so disastrously out of character
for Rose that it would draw more attention than the smoking itself.

So Rose smoked in the student carpark. It was situated
a comforting distance from the administration block and
was bordered by a patch of unkempt bush populated by
magpies and dumped rubbish. Incongruously termed the
School Nature Strip, it was avoided by everyone out of fear
of swoopers and snakes.

Rose would squat by the bumper of a parked car to
smoke and then flick her butts into the scrub.

She smoked as many cigarettes as she could when she
was there. Not just one, but three, sometimes four, back to
back, sucked down head-spinningly fast. She would spray
herself with Impulse after each tobacco binge and chew
gum until her jaw ached.

Still, she had seen her mum smelling her laundry as she
sorted it. She had seen Michael's dad at church turn towards
her, inhaling with furrowed brow. She didn't care.

When Michael sniffed Rose's hair, she pretended it was a
romantic gesture even though he squinted and looked sad.
When Michael had dinner at Rose's and her mum dipped

her head coquettishly to one side and remarked, "Michael, I think you might be smoking," he'd said yes without really thinking about it and because he loved Rose.

Rose was scaring Michael lately too. She was becoming all sharp edges. It wasn't just the weight loss. Michael had studied cross-section diagrams of pregnancy in all its mysterious stages. From a kidney bean smudge curled up in tight folds of rigid muscle to a bona fide thing just like you saw in prams on the street, getting so big it shoved internal organs out of the way as if it were building a snow cave.

Rose's ability to drag her body with her into plausible deniability should have made Michael shudder with euphoric relief, but it didn't. He began to feel sick, like he had on the day she first told him she was pregnant. Her face was beginning to sink into her skull. She looked bloodless and parched.

And something else was happening. Rose was twitchy and strident. Michael would sometimes hear her braying clear across the quadrangle. He would look at her and her skin shone like beached cuttlefish.

When they spent time together she wouldn't speak of it.

"You look sick."

"I don't know what you mean," Rose would answer, always with a cadence of finality.

Just like Michael's mum. *If I say it, it will come to be. I speak my reality and so create yours. No correspondence will be entered into.*

Except Michael never expected to be excluded from the truth along with everybody else.

He wasn't sleeping well. Was Rose? He wondered if that

nascent snow-caver ever sent tendrils of sadness into Rose's dreams. It lived in his. It pulsed and rolled and nudged like a manatee in his spinal fluid, and it wasn't even growing in him.

He wanted to ask Rose how she did it. But he knew she would answer, "Do what?"

The week before school holidays two students were expelled for stealing a car and one fainted during a mock exam. Teachers began the precarious balancing act between propitious maneuvering of their charges towards school and personal success, and unconcealed joy that another year of dragging combative no-hopers towards academic mediocrity was almost over. Students were advised to use their holidays wisely, as the last term would come and go relatively fast.

The last term was coming, and Michael could feel it.

Michael knew he was being scrutinized. Fortunately the stinging panic that had sat like a film on his eyeballs ever since the kidney bean first appeared was erroneously identified by everyone around him as exam prep anxiety. Exam prep anxiety became Michael's panacea. The askance squint he developed was mistaken for eye strain, the teeth grinding for concentration, the silences for meditative study, and fatigue for long days and nights of preparing to fulfill everyone's expectations.

There was an uncomfortable consolation in this for Michael. He could pull a little peace from temporary acceptance of his erraticism even while knowing it could never last.

This was the eye of the storm, and Michael knew it.

14

Michael and Rose usually sat together in church. Sometimes they would sit with his family, sometimes they would sit with hers.

When they stood to sing the hymns, Michael would just mouth the words so he could listen to Rose's voice. He loved the swell of it. She made the hairs on his arms stand up. He once told Rose that her singing in church was like a pulse in a room full of corpses. She said "Ewww" in response, so he didn't try explaining any further. He just listened.

Every now and then some elderly parishioner with a voice like a foghorn would stand behind Michael and belt out the hymns, swallowing up Rose's voice in an airstream of must and denture adhesive. It had always irritated him, but lately it made him so extremely angry that he would have to breathe slowly and grip the back of the pew in front of him just to stop himself from turning around and screaming, "Shut the fuck up!"

He had fantasies about it. He would imagine the slow turn to face the perpetrator, the slight faltering of their song as they recognized rage in his face, the inhalation of air that would carry that rage out of his chest and throat, and the release of the scream. It made him happy to think about it.

Today they were sitting with his family and there was no elderly foghorn behind them. Michael was disappointed not to have the distraction of his rage to get through the sermon.

Instead he decided to study the small girl squatting on the floor between pews coloring in. It was one of those Dream-Works coloring-in books based on some feature-length cartoon. He couldn't place the characters. He knew he recognized them, but he couldn't remember the name of the movie. This irritated him too.

Then, when she began to color outside the lines, Michael felt his anger build until he wanted to lean over and snatch the pencil out of her hand. He imagined her struggling to hold onto it and having to break a finger or two to prise it out of her hand. He imagined the girl screaming, her mother screaming, her father grabbing him and slamming him into a wall, the entire congregation turning, aghast, with wide eyes and hands over mouths. His own father looking at him as if he were a stranger.

Then the relief came. That little bit of relief he could only access through rage. It never lasted long enough.

He looked at the girl again. She wasn't even trying to get it right. Just scribbling over Fiona's face, ruining the page.

Shrek. That was it. *Shrek.*

Michael and Rose got out of the church as quickly as possible after the service. They used to hang around, mingle, accept and answer questions from well-intentioned old people, friends of their parents, elders of the church. They used to get involved in the youth group, help organize safe group outings to safe venues where the boys and girls could pair off safely and flirt and kiss. They used to join their parents in the church hall after service for a cup of tea and a piece of dry cake donated by some woman who received far more gratitude for her efforts than was deserved.

But now they just got out of there as quickly as possible. They would sit together on the limestone wall that bordered the carpark and hold hands and not say very much at all.

Sometimes they didn't hold hands. Michael would say something like, "How are you?" and Rose would say, "Good," and Michael would say, "Not feeling sick or anything?" and Rose would say, "Why would I be feeling sick?" and Michael would feel like crying. Or breaking a little girl's fingers.

Sunday was family day in Michael's house. It always had been. After church they would go home and there would be a roast, even on hot days, and in the evening a light dinner of sandwiches stuffed with leftover roast drizzled with coagulated leftover gravy. There would be homework to do and usually a football game on TV. Michael's mum would do the ironing.

It wasn't that they spent every minute of the day together. It was just an understanding that they would share their time and tasks in a kind of family bubble. Guests were unusual on a Sunday. Phone calls, in or out, were rare.

Michael used to love Sundays, but now they seemed too quiet. He began to long for a neighbor to mow a lawn, just so he could concentrate on some white noise other than the thrumming in his own head. He couldn't study, couldn't follow the football, couldn't hear what people were saying to him.

His father began to get annoyed, and motivated, by having to say everything twice to Michael just to extract a response. And the one thing Michael dreaded was his father's motivation to pay more attention to these subtle changes in behavior that Michael could neither control nor predict.

It was on a Sunday that Michael and his father had their first fight. They had disagreed before, but the outcome of any disagreement in Michael's house was preordained. Years of modeling by their mother had taught both Michael and Tim that backing down and thanking their father for pointing out the flaws in their own thinking was the most productive course to take in any difference of opinion. Michael not only accepted this, but he also believed his father to be right.

Recently, however, his mother's acquiescence had begun to smell like submission. And without a neighbor's lawn-mower to meditate upon, his father's approach began to smack of bullying.

The fight started with this: "Michael, I don't like repeating myself."

This worried Michael immediately, because if his father had already repeated himself and didn't like it, then he was bound to be hacked off at having to say whatever he didn't like repeating yet again.

Michael considered trying to wing it and pretend he had heard, but the possibilities were numerous and whatever his father had said might require follow-up action which Michael couldn't possibly wing.

He could hear his mother humming at the ironing board.

"Sorry, Dad. I am listening."

"And now you're lying to me as well," his father said.

And there was the trap. Michael was familiar with it. His "I am listening" had just slipped out. He hadn't thought it through, and it was a lie. But it was a lie of preservation in the face of being set up.

He began to think about all the ways his father set him up. Set them all up.

His father was inordinately calm. It occurred to Michael that his father might be enjoying this.

"No, Dad. I'm not lying. I wasn't listening before, but I'm listening now."

"Don't play games with me, Michael," his father said, shifting slightly in his chair. He was reading the paper, or pretending to. He didn't take his eyes off the page, just shifted ever so slightly, making the paper creak as he adjusted his center of gravity.

Michael knew that tactic as well. It used to terrify him as a boy. His father was preparing to get up. *If he had to.*

"I don't think Michael meant anything," his mother said, her voice rising to an edgy chirp.

"Not really your business, Maureen. And we don't really know what Michael means these days, do we, Michael? We know he doesn't listen and we know he lies about it. We don't know much else. I think it's time we put some strategies in place to get you back on track, young man. For a start, no more after-school activities. Once you've been accepted into medicine you can do whatever you want, but for now we'll see if a more disciplined approach to life can help your hearing problem."

"Okay," Michael said.

He didn't care. What his father didn't know was that Michael had dropped his after-school activities weeks ago. He spent those hours after school sitting under a tree on the school oval with Rose, talking about natural disasters and terrorist attacks. He had read somewhere that whenever there was a loss of life on a massive scale there were some people who used the opportunity as a cover to begin a new life. They disappeared, their remains were assumed pulverized, and they simply wandered off to begin their new life with a brand-new identity.

Michael desperately wanted to be assumed pulverized.

"Okay?" His father slowly lowered the newspaper and looked intently at Michael over the top of his glasses. "Okay? Don't you care about your after-school activities? Because if you don't, I can think of something you do care about."

"I don't think Michael meant — "

"Shut up, Maureen!"

Something happened then. Michael knew he wasn't playing his father's game by the rules. He was supposed to affect remorse and disappointment at the loss of these after-school privileges and then thank his father for giving him the opportunity to do better by graciously accepting his punishment.

But Michael didn't want to. He liked the risk of infuriating his father. He wanted to take control of something, of anything.

So he said, "Take whatever you want, Dad. I don't care. And don't tell Mum to shut up."

Michael said all this quietly but clearly, looking directly at his father.

His father's eyes popped open as if someone had smashed a plate behind him. Shock, followed by fury at being shocked.

"I think you're spending too much time with Rose," his father said, slowly standing up. "And I've heard she's started smoking. Her lack of personal discipline is obviously a bad influence on you. You're not to see Rose until after your exams. End of discussion."

His father began lowering himself back into his recliner just as Michael began to stand. For just a second Michael was struck by the comedy of it. It was as if he and his father were on a seesaw. *Up, down, up, down.* If he jumped off at the right time he could crack his father's coccyx with so much force he'd feel it in his teeth.

"No," Michael said, his heart thrashing like a kitten in a sack. "I'll see Rose when I want to. I love her."

He turned and was about to walk out of the room when his father started to laugh. A hard-edged, sour guffaw that hit Michael in the back of the throat like a swig of vinegar.

This is it, Michael thought. *This is the taste of being mocked.*

"You," his father managed to gulp out between breaths, "don't even know what love is."

Michael lunged so quickly at his father that he managed to land one good punch before it was over.

And it was over quickly. Michael's father twisted Michael's arm up behind his back, forced him face down onto the carpet and pinioned him into position with a knee to the small of his back.

His mother screamed. Tim bolted into the room. Mi-

chael could hear Tim pleading with their father to let him
go; he could hear his mother crying; he could smell something burning.

Had his mother left the iron face down on a shirt again?
Michael hoped it was one of his mother's blouses burning.
Dad always got so mad when she scorched one of his work
shirts.

He could feel his lungs burning — was that what he
could smell? — as his father increased the pressure on his
back. He was biting the inside of his cheek and he could
taste the blood.

Then it was over. His father was off him, staggering backwards. Michael rolled over onto his back, looked up at the
ceiling and began to laugh. He laughed up at his father with
such gusto that he sprayed blood from his mouth.

From that angle his father just looked like an appalled
old man. Michael had gotten off the seesaw at just the right
moment.

15

Michael realized that attracting attention through dissension was a mistake, even though he lived off the adrenaline of laughing at his father for days after the incident. He recognized the madness within himself that Sunday. Recognized its little tap dance on his heart and on his tongue.

But he couldn't let it loose again.

When Michael told Rose about it, she didn't understand. She didn't understand Michael's joy at having bested his father, as he saw it, nor was she pleased at the shift this portended in Michael's relationship with him.

She wanted things to stay the same. The way they always had been. There was no reason why they shouldn't.

Rose was also becoming antsy about the fact that she and Michael weren't having sex as often. The last time they tried, Michael noticed the tight swelling above her pubis. It was firm and obvious when Rose was naked, and Michael ran his fingers across it until Rose slapped his hand away.

Then she cried.

"I'm sorry," was the only thing he could think to say, and that sounded hopeless and insincere.

Rose rolled onto her side away from Michael and sobbed, "You don't understand," which was, Michael had to admit, perfectly accurate.

Rose wanted sex all the time now and even insisted on Michael using a condom, which Michael told her was like closing the barn door after the horse had bolted, which made Rose cry even more because she didn't know what it meant.

Michael got up and dressed, watching Rose's shoulders twitch and shake. He couldn't get close to her for the very same reason she needed the closeness so badly. Neither of them knew what it meant.

Rose eventually sat up, leaky eyed, and lit a cigarette.

"You're smoking in the house?" Michael was appalled. "Your mum will smell it. You'll get busted."

"She smells it." Rose inhaled deeply and used the heel of her hand to wipe a smear of mucus from her upper lip. "She pretends she can't smell it and I pretend I don't smoke. Works for everyone."

"What about your dad?"

"Dad smells what Mum tells him he smells. When he's around, that is."

Michael sat on the edge of the bed. He took the cigarette gently from Rose's fingers and dropped it into a half-empty can of Red Bull on the bedside table.

"I love you," he said.

"I know. I love you too."

When Rose was caught smoking by Miss Douglas on the

first day of the last term, she found herself in the unhappy position of being the one giving comfort.

Rose had been in Miss Douglas's English class three years prior and liked her enormously. Rose had great potential. Miss Douglas had said so. Several times.

So when Miss Douglas sidled around the Volkswagen bug Rose was squatting behind and saw Rose on her haunches mid-drag, her face collapsed into a disappointment that hit Rose like a backhander.

"Not *you*, Rose. Anyone but you."

Rose didn't stand up quickly in a flurry of guilty fidget, as might have been expected. Her lack of urgency made Miss Douglas slump against the side of the car and drop her bottom lip just enough to make Rose think she might cry.

Rose took another long drag before slowly standing up, limbs unfolding like a stick insect, and flicking her butt into the underbrush.

"It's all right, Miss Douglas," she said, each word in a robe of smoke. "Don't worry."

"Get in there and stand on that thing or you'll start a fire. Then come with me."

They sat opposite each other in an empty classroom, Miss Douglas all fretful disappointment and Rose just a bit confused as to the fuss.

Rose liked this room. It was the one the drama department used for read-throughs. It was a little darker today, blinds closed fast against the promise of unseasonal heat, ceiling fans fluttering the corners of school-production posters, whiteboard blushing blue from erratic erasures.

It was like a stage. Womb-quiet, just the faraway hum of

students at lunch like an audience in pre-curtain anticipation. Miss Douglas and Rose the mummers, just traveling through briefly and only to entertain each other.

Rose wondered if she could get out of this chair and sit on the floor instead. She felt more comfortable closer to the ground these days.

"There'll have to be a letter home to your parents. That's procedure. But what I'm most concerned about, Rose, is that this just isn't like you." Miss Douglas waited for Rose to confirm the incongruity.

Rose felt she had to give her something, so she smiled the smile of someone choosing the emotion most likely to placate. She imagined herself holding out an ice cream to a small sad child.

"It's all right, Miss Douglas."

"No, Rose. It's not all right. Something's not right."

"That's not what I meant exactly," Rose said, leaning forward slightly to confirm her commitment to the business at hand. "I know I shouldn't have been smoking. I don't even know why I was. I won't do it again. Really."

"I hope not, Rose. It's just not like you."

Rose realized that she didn't appear to be who she was anymore and that this was far more disquieting to Miss Douglas than the cigarette itself. Rose had forced a perception shift on Miss Douglas and all that was required was for Rose to reassure this teacher that she, Rose, was indeed who she was, this anomalous incident notwithstanding.

"You don't look well either, Rose. You've lost weight, you're pale ..."

"I have a virus in me."

Rose heard herself interrupt a little more shrilly than she had intended and had to smile because it was funny.

"What sort of virus?"

"The sort that makes me thin and pale?"

Rose immediately regretted saying it. Miss Douglas looked hurt. She was trying to help.

"Miss Douglas, I'm sorry. I've been a bit sick, and exams and stuff are …" She trailed off.

It occurred to Rose that she was going to have to be more careful. She was going to have to find the balance between vigilantly fighting the virus and not drawing attention to herself.

Like being in the school play. She would stand before the crowd, footlights warming her toes, as the audience's eyes adjusted to the darkness and saw not her but the character represented by her chosen costume. The character embedded in Rose, the costume permeating her skin, her fiction soaking right down to her organs. Deep into her, even to the virus.

People see but they do not see.

"Rose, is there anything you want to talk about?"

"No."

"Do you want to talk to someone else?"

"No."

Miss Douglas leaned back then and looked around the room. She herself remembered the pressures of final exams. This was a time for students to go a bit crazy. And stress-related illness was not uncommon.

Still, something didn't feel right here.

"When's your guidance counselor interview?"

"This week. Wednesday, I think."

"Okay." Miss Douglas stood then. "You need to take care of yourself, Rose. You need to get rid of this virus and start thinking about your future. And a letter will be going home to your parents about this. That's all."

Rose recognized, with gratitude, the dismissal.

When Rose stepped onto the verandah, the heat hit her. Liv was sitting on a bench just outside. They didn't speak.

Rose always brought the mail in after school for her parents.

Rose had been looking forward to the interview with the guidance counselor. She needed application information for drama school. She wouldn't be applying immediately. She knew she would have to work for a while, put some money aside, and maybe buy a car, but she wanted to be prepared and the anticipation of that preparation made her feel happier than she had in weeks.

She was surprised to see Miss Douglas coming out of the office just before she herself was due to go in. She smiled warmly, genuinely at Miss Douglas.

Miss Douglas touched her on the shoulder as she walked past.

When Rose was seated in front of the counselor she launched immediately into her plans. She found herself distracted by the fact that the counselor kept scratching her own armpit, but Rose was determined to get all the information she needed.

The counselor began rummaging for pamphlets and

contact information while Rose outlined her two-year plan.

"I'll work for a while, of course, and take drama classes. But my main goal is to be prepared for auditions by this time next year."

"It's good to see someone who has a real plan, Rose." Sigh. "Here is all the information about the schools you're interested in. Entrance criteria, course information. That sort of thing. And you're not finding the last term stressful at all?"

Rose didn't respond immediately. She suddenly felt unfocused and had to pull herself back into the room and re-settle her edges.

"Rose? Are you having any trouble with your last term?"

"No, no, not at all. I'm just excited."

"Well, good. That's good." Scratch. "Come back if you need anything else. Okay?"

Rose bumped into Tiffany and Holly on the way to her next class, and they shrieked with excitement as she showed them the school brochures. She linked arms with Holly as she walked past Liv.

16

Liv waited for Michael in the skate park after school. She knew he got off the bus and walked across the park to get home. She cut the last two classes of the day just to make sure she got there before him. It wasn't cold but she found herself crawling with gooseflesh.

It was still called the skate park even though the cement bowl that had once been used for that purpose had long since been filled in and grassed over and was now just a dimple in the earth covered with recycled rubber matting and a swing set.

There were a couple of brick barbecues near the perimeter that no one ever used and two enormous trees that had been cordoned off with caution tape after they were ringbarked. The city was trying to save them. There had been articles in the local paper about tree doctors performing emergency grafts in order to pull the trees back from the brink.

The caution tape made the park look like a crime scene. Liv and Rose used to come to the skate park regularly to see if the trees were healing.

Michael didn't see Liv immediately when he got off the bus. As usual when one was not expecting to see the unexpected, his attention was selectively drawn to only those things that were familiar to him. The playground with the dark, spongy surface Michael thought must have looked like a giant thumbprint from space. The barbecues that were now just altars to bird shit. The caution tape barricading the trees he and Ryan had ringbarked last summer for a bet.

Liv was sitting at the same picnic table Rose had been on the day she slapped him. When Michael saw her, he felt a rush of déjà vu quickly followed by the urge to turn and walk in the other direction. He was suddenly and utterly fraught but, despite the desire not to, found himself moving steadily towards her.

He'd decided to walk straight past Liv, when she climbed off the table, intercepting him with, "Mind if we have a chat?"

Michael did mind. He minded a great deal. His lip curled. "What do you want?"

"I want to talk to you about Rose."

"Well, I don't want to talk to you."

Michael was walking past her when she said, "I know she's pregnant. She says she's not, but I know she is." And when Michael didn't stop, "I told my mum."

Michael stopped then and he turned to face Liv. He didn't know if she was telling the truth or not, but either way he was rapidly feeling a loss of control in this situation.

He dropped his backpack and took a step towards her before saying again, "What do you want?"

"I want to know what you're going to do about it. She's

making herself sick. She won't talk to me. I thought maybe
…"

"You thought maybe what?"

"I thought maybe you could talk to her for me. I want to help."

Michael laughed. A dropstitch of breaths hard with sarcasm.

"Let me bring you up to speed," he said. "You don't know shit. And even if you did no one would believe a word you said. You're just a sad slag dumped by the only friend you ever had. No one else talks to you, do they? Not even your boyfriends, before, during or after. Especially after."

Liv had never really spoken to Michael before. They had shared insignificant banter on occasion and exchanged nods and smiles in the hallway when he was with Rose. She had made certain assumptions about him because Rose loved him and she loved Rose.

But now she was suddenly dizzy with adrenaline and when she tried to swallow she had no spit.

Michael was stepping away from her and picking up his backpack.

Liv rushed forward and without really thinking shoved him in the back before saying, "What the *fuck*?"

He staggered forward but didn't lose his balance. Liv was shortwinded by the exertion and making small noises as she exhaled.

"You … you …"

"I *what*?" he bawled.

He turned to face her, moved closer to her and dropped his voice to a hoarse monotone.

"She's not pregnant. She's not sick. She's not your business."

Michael looked at Liv carefully. He looked in her startled eyes and then traced the perimeter of her face with his own.

She was much smaller than he had thought. How was his perception of her so screwed? He thought she was taller than this, had more meat on her bones. But she was tiny. She must have put a lot of mettle into that shove.

Then Liv said, "Rose is my friend," in a croaky, exhausted kind of way, and Michael knew he was back in control of this conversation.

"You are not Rose's friend. You are a dirty little parasite with daddy issues. And you can tell that white-trash mother of yours anything you want. Just try and get her between tokes."

Michael didn't turn from Liv straight away. He held her gaze, surprised to find her holding his.

Then, unexpectedly, Liv moved in. Michael couldn't explain it, but that tall, well-muscled perception of Liv that Michael saw flounced so thoroughly by his vilification suddenly returned, moved in behind her eyes even as he watched them. It would have been imperceptible from across a room, even from arm's length. A small hardening, a tiny self-satisfied turn of the mouth, and her palm resting flat against his chest.

Michael didn't even realize she had reached out to touch him until the touch landed.

"Why are you so angry, Michael? This isn't about me at all, is it? Still going to marry her, Michael?" Liv dropped her hand to her side before saying, "Has she miscarried?"

Michael dropped his eyes then. Liv stared at his forehead and waited.

"Michael?"

"What?"

"Has she miscarried?"

"I don't … I'm not sure. Probably."

"*Probably?* Michael, you'd know if she miscarried. She'd bleed like a fucking stuck pig!"

They stood together, heads bowed slightly, in such a way that from a distance it might appear as if they were friends. Michael felt so comfortably detached from everything in that moment, that he believed he could stay standing in uncomfortable silence with this girl he hated forever. Little vacuum of nothingness.

He remembered how easy it had been to girdle those trees. He could even remember the smell of the living tree flesh.

"Okay," Liv said coolly. "Here's the thing, Michael. You're pissing off the only person who gives a fuck. Do you get that? I'm Rosie's friend."

It was the gentle conversational tone that made Michael look up at Liv.

"Being accidentally knocked-up is not the end of the goddamn world. But the bullshit you two are running just might be. I can't believe I was jealous."

"Jealous?"

Michael wanted Liv to be jealous. He wanted her to envy Rose, to envy him.

"Yeah, jealous. Crazy shit." Liv laughed and said, "You see, Rose told me you loved her. I guess that was the least dodgy of her delusions."

Liv turned then and began to walk away. She crossed the park and got to the street counting her own steps.

When she reached the pavement she turned back. Michael was sitting at the picnic table between the caution tape and the swing set. His backpack was on the ground and his head was in his hands. He looked as if he were praying.

And Liv decided she was staying out of it.

17

The least dodgy of her delusions.

Michael couldn't get the phrase out of his head. He tried not to think about it but somehow hearing Liv say it out loud had snapped him back into reality with a whip-cracking shock. He had to sit down on the bench next to the picnic table and resist the desire to scream.

And he knew he had to talk to Rose. Really talk to Rose. He had to sit down with her and drag her through the bramble of whatever fantasy it was that kept her unthinkingly functional while he himself was close to falling apart.

They had decisions to make. Because despite Rose's protestations and Michael's prayers, it wasn't going away as they had imagined it might. Michael had seen Rose using a safety pin to secure the zipper on a favorite skirt because the zipper teeth no longer met.

He called Rose from the park but she didn't answer.

During the walk home Michael began to wonder if he should tell Tim. He knew his only motivation for doing so would be to feel the relief of having the knowledge shared.

He knew Tim would keep his secret. He also knew there was absolutely nothing Tim could do to help.

Help. It was the sort of word that was usually screamed. It was the sort of need that usually required screaming. People yelled help when there was a fire or they were injured or someone was attacking them. Other people responded quickly and efficiently to this yelling.

But a whispered help, that was different. Whispered helps were full of secrets and shameful desperation. Rather than halve the burden, a whispered help would divide the crisis and let it gain strength and complexity — a sort of emotional mitosis. Not unlike passing a disease on to the one trying to save you. And if nothing would change as a result of the whisper anyway, if all it would do was bring about the inevitable outcome, only sooner, then why bother? *Better just to fall down and wait, wasn't it?*

When Michael got home he knew something was wrong. His father was sitting in the recliner by the bookshelf, his reading chair, with no book. This in itself was not particularly alarming. However, the precise way in which he was tracing the pleat in his trousers with the corner of the envelope he was holding was.

Up and down, up and down, accompanied by the *swish, swish* of the thick paper against wool-polyester blend, like a razor against a strop.

"Do you know what I have here?" his father began.

Michael dropped his backpack but did not respond.

"I have a letter from school. It asks for confirmation that you were absent from school with parental permission on Monday, Wednesday afternoon and Thursday morning of last week."

Michael knew that at any moment he would be asked for an explanation. He had been expecting this to catch up with him sooner or later.

How could he explain to his father that each absence had been absolutely necessary? On each of those occasions he had been sick and tired. He was feeling sick and tired now.

Why did people diminish that phrase? It was the perfect description for the sort of seasickness that wallowed behind his eyes more and more. He had timed two of those absences to coincide with hours he knew his mother was out of the house and had snuck home and gone to bed. He seemed to sleep better during the day lately for some reason.

Michael braced himself for the booming reprimand and demand for an account of his whereabouts, but it didn't come. Instead his father got out of his chair and walked slowly towards Michael until they were face to face.

Michael went to take a step backwards but his father grabbed his upper arm. He leaned in so close their noses touched. Incongruously, Michael found himself wanting to laugh and squeezed his bladder tight to try to prevent it.

"Don't disappoint me," his father whispered. "I won't brook it. Do not humiliate me again."

He let go then, pushing Michael back just enough to cause a stagger and awkward recovery against the door-frame.

That was it. Michael thought about bending down to retrieve his backpack but was afraid he would fall over.

His father walked away then, turning back briefly to say, "I called the school. Told them you were sick."

Rose saw the missed call from Michael and went to her room to call him back.

"Do you want to come over for dinner?" she said immediately upon his greeting.

"Not really."

"Come on," she pleaded. "You haven't been over for dinner for ages. Didn't see you much at school today. I hate Thursdays. I missed you. Anything much happen today? I had my history mock-up. I'm going to ace that exam."

Small talk. Ordinary and chirpy. Chirpy like a bird. Alert like a bird in a frenetic escape from a predator.

"Mum's going out later," Rose singsonged. "We'd have the place to ourselves."

"Is your dad away again? Didn't he just get back?"

"He was back for a month."

A month? Rose's father had been back a month and was gone again already? Michael hadn't seen him once. Had a month passed? Longer, even?

Time seemed to be moving without taking Michael and Rose along with it.

"So," Rose continued, "come for dinner. Come for ... whatever you want."

Come for whatever you want.

Trouble was, Michael didn't want it anymore. He couldn't bend his perception the way Rose seemed to be able to.

Her body had changed. Beneath all those tracksuit pants and baggy T-shirts she had taken to wearing like a uniform, her torso had become as tight and shiny as a giant hornet's sting. There were swellings everywhere.

Michael thought about telling Rose about his fight with

Liv, thought about telling her about his fight with his father, thought about telling her about his fight with himself.

Instead he said, "I can't come for dinner."

Rose felt herself tensing. It wasn't just the words. It was the tone. There was a sadness in it that she had seen and heard in Michael often lately.

"So why did you call?" she asked.

Rose felt sad sometimes too. She felt sad about not sleeping in her mother's bed anymore. Sleeping in her mother's bed, even when her mother wasn't in it, was comforting. Like being held. And because the purpose of going to bed was to sleep, there was no expectation for conversation and Rose was able to rest there, beside her mother's breathing. The darkness of her mother's nighttime room was like fingers in Rose's hair — the only time of the day she need not comfort her mother with the reflection of a happy home shining like a well-polished mirror in her tired face.

Now Rose slept in her own bed every night on sheets that were patchy with crust that smelled of Michael. Her mother had left fresh linen on the end of Rose's bed. She usually changed the linen for Rose but she'd stopped doing that. She didn't ask why Rose had stopped crawling into her bed either.

Rose couldn't risk it. She couldn't risk her mother feeling something besides Rose moving in the night.

"Michael?" Rose said when the silence on the other end of the phone began crackling like static. "Michael, why did you call?"

"Do you know what we're going to do?" Michael asked quickly.

"About what?"

"I love you," Michael replied, before hanging up.

The least dodgy of her delusions.

18

Rose missed Michael. A fraught status quo seemed to exist between them. It was as if each of them was precariously balanced over an enormous drop, an abyss that neither of them would mention even while it caused their voices to echo and the tiny patches of workable ground beneath them to crumble. He wasn't coming around as much and he seemed preoccupied.

So when he suggested they go to a movie, she skipped a play rehearsal to do so. She was as giddily excited about the date as she had been those first few times they had spent alone together. Those times when she used to take extra care with her appearance, when she'd get the hair straightener out and agonize over wardrobe choices and let Liv do her makeup just for fun before washing it off and starting again because Liv always made her look like a hooker just for fun.

Rose held dresses and jeans up against her body in front of the full-length mirror on the back of her bedroom door and twirled a bit, and sometimes in her peripheral vision she imagined Liv sitting on the end of her bed chugging

Diet Coke and exclaiming, "More eyeliner, woman!" as Rose did own her makeup.

When she was ready, Liv would always say, "You look beautiful," and Rose would know she meant it.

Rose eventually chose a pair of black stretch pants and a black satin A-line shift dress that fell to her knees. Her mother knocked on the door occasionally, almost as excited as Rose herself, just to see if Rose needed any help getting ready.

It had been a long time since Rose had made an effort to dress up and go out, and Violet was thrilled and relieved with this sudden return of enthusiasm to her daughter. She even obliged when Rose asked for a couple of ibuprofen. Violet didn't want niggling back pain to ruin Rose and Michael's first proper date in months.

Michael was late picking up Rose. The short walk to her place was almost thwarted at the first step when his father bailed him up about where he was going. Michael told a lie, which was not believed, yet accepted. The only thing holding Michael together these days was a caul of lies that by this time had dried hard and set his face in a grimace.

Rose noticed that face when she opened her front door but refused to give in to it. They walked to the bus stop and sat down.

"We need to talk," Michael said. "Well, I need to talk."

"Okay." Rose took Michael's hand.

"I don't think I can do this," Michael continued.

"Do what?" Rose replied.

Michael moaned then. He let his head loll backwards and looked straight up into the slowly darkening sky.

Streetlights were just beginning to flicker to life. People were walking by.

"You're pregnant."

It was the first time the words had actually been used since that day in Rose's bedroom, so long ago now and yet as resonant as the second that had just passed.

He turned to look at her then and she was smiling — tremulous and meager, but a smile just the same. Her eyelid began to twitch.

Michael envied in Rose what appeared to be a lesser struggle. His own fear of discovery was beginning to cause a rot from within. It was like waking in the middle of the night to find one arm asleep, experiencing that moment of horror at being attached to a dead thing.

"No, no," Rose began.

Michael could hear the excitement in her voice.

"Something's happened," she continued. "I have period pain, and today … today there was some blood." She was fidgety with the thrill of the news. "I was right, Michael. I was right all along. I don't think it was ever there. Not really. I just created this thing in my mind, you see. It's not real."

"Rose." Michael said her name and nothing more.

Rose began to cry then, smile and cry and twitch, exhilarated by the deep cramping she knew was the start of her period. She was frightened that Michael didn't believe her. Frightened by how her own body had deceived her for this long.

Here she was, finally rational and back in control, and Michael was cutting the rope that tied his raft to hers.

"Michael, the bus."

But Michael didn't get up and neither did Rose.

Michael wondered if Rose could be right. He allowed himself a moment to consider the possibility that they had both been caught up in a sort of blind hysteria. He wanted that to be true.

He thought about the book they had read in English: *The War of the Worlds*. They had talked about the dramatization of the book on radio, and how people had believed an invasion was happening simply because they were being told an invasion was happening. A story about the sublimation of the human race had sublimated the human race. Not for long, but long enough to create useless panic.

He looked at Rose. Her hand, fingers intertwined with his, gripped him a bit too tightly. He wanted her to let go. She was so pale. She looked like a little girl. He knew then that any panic he was feeling was justified.

"Did you pick a movie?" he asked her.

"No. What do you want to see?"

"Decide when we get there?"

"Okay."

Michael put his arm around Rose and pulled her into him. They were reciprocally connected in the maintenance of a secret that Rose no longer believed to be true even as it grew wings inside her.

Counterbalancing each other, breathing in unison, they waited for the next bus.

19

Liv sent texts to Rose, which went unanswered.

Rose took each text like an arrow. Her fingers would dawdle over the phone, ghosting a response, imagining Liv's mother-touch, remembering that safe place.

Then Rose's belly would itch and she would be afraid again and so delete Liv's message.

But there was one message Rose didn't delete: I'll always be here for u.

It was sent at the end of outdoor ed class.

Rose had successfully avoided outdoor ed for three months. She'd had pulled muscles from playing squash on the weekend, migraines, diarrhea, her period every two weeks, and sometimes she simply didn't turn up.

She'd been spoken to about her absences several times but had shown sufficient study-anxiety-related remorse for her behavior to so far successfully avoid any real scrutiny.

But scrutiny did come when she lolled outside the change rooms sans bathing suit yet again and calmly explained to Mrs. Shaw that she had bad period pain.

"You had your period last week, Rose."

Had she? Rose was losing track of time.

She smiled awkwardly because she couldn't think of anything to say. She needed rehearsal time.

"I really do have bad cramps, Mrs. Shaw."

"Just go back in there and change, Rose," Mrs. Shaw continued. "You've got five minutes. I want you in the pool."

Rose returned to the change rooms and sat down on one of the long wooden benches, leaning back against a locker. She closed her eyes but found that without a visual rouser the smell in the room was almost unbearable. Chlorine and towels that smelled like wet dog, sweat and the sickly afterburn of dozens of aerosol deodorants sprayed day in and day out, all competed in air that was too moist and warm.

Rose opened her eyes and waited for a swell of briny nausea to pass. She wished she hadn't used her period as an excuse so often. Now, when it was finally forming like an iron cairn inside her, no one believed her.

She grabbed her bag and walked out.

Class was in full session. Teachers barked from the edge of the pool, girls dutifully completed laps, others sat in tight groups under sun sails, stretching their lithe limbs and giggling. Rose used to be one of them. She could see Liv standing by herself near the bleachers, one hand pressed to her forehead in a salute against the sun, other hand on hip.

With everyone occupied, Rose made her way quickly to the gate. She was almost out of sight when she heard Mrs. Shaw.

"Stop right there!"

When Rose turned, she saw she was not the only one startled by the order. Several others nearby had also stopped and turned to look. A light breeze caught her T-shirt, so she pressed her bag in front of her. She saw Liv making her way slowly around the pool.

"I didn't excuse you, Rose," Mrs. Shaw continued. "Where are you going?"

"I don't … nowhere … home."

Each tiny word Rose said was snatched up by the breeze. She couldn't get any volume up, couldn't fill her lungs enough to make herself heard over the hubbub.

"What?" Mrs. Shaw started walking towards Rose. Everyone was looking now. Mrs. Shaw approached from one side of the pool. Liv continued easing her way towards Rose from the other. The pincer maneuver skillfully executed just prior to an attack.

Rose began to back up, a strange panic making her skin tingle with heat.

Then Mrs. Shaw was there in front of her like a bulwark. Rose couldn't look at her.

"Liv, go back to what you were doing," Mrs. Shaw said, noticing Liv loitering at the flank. "This isn't your business."

Liv didn't move away. She waited, staring directly at Rose.

"I said, *Where are you going, Rose?*"

Rose stared down at her own forearms clutching her bag to her body. She had to get out of there. She had to leave, now. She could feel herself burning with the need of it.

She traced the spaces between arm freckles with wet eyes and said, "I don't feel well."

That's when Mrs. Shaw placed a hand, feather light, on Rose's arm and said, "Let's have a talk."

It was the touch that did it. It might just as well have been a tourniquet of barbed wire.

Rose yanked her arm back, spinning her body.

Liv stepped forward, convinced Rose was going to lose her balance.

Rose looked Mrs. Shaw hard in the eye and said, "Don't touch me."

Mrs. Shaw opened her mouth but didn't speak. Behind her, the laps had stopped. Students bobbed in the lanes, or leaned on the edges of the pool, their tentacle-legs waving just below the water's surface.

A swim coach had emerged from the small office to the side of the change room. He made two steps towards the trio. Rose needed no further motivation to bolt.

She ran from the pool, up the small grassy incline that led away from the school. She skirted the hockey field, vaguely aware of the hoot and holler of those in the midst of a game, ran past the student carpark, past the groundskeeper sheds, watched the street being pulled closer and closer to her by pure will and pounding feet.

When she reached the street she kept going, the elation of escape overriding the burning in her calves and the ache in her lower back. She ran two blocks uphill in the direction of the ocean before collapsing into a bus shelter and vomiting on the pavement.

She sat in the bus shelter, oblivious to the vomit on her shoes, and cried.

When her phone chirruped she dug it out of her bag and read the text from Liv.

I'll always be here for u.

20

The back pain was a welcome distraction. It wasn't a sharp pain so much as a dull, drawing ache like a fishhook in the base of her spine being occasionally tugged. Sometimes the tugging went on for a long time and Rose began to imagine herself rising in the water, rushing towards the light of a clear blue sky against the cold pressure of an opposing current.

And then the tugging would subside and she would just bob about beneath the surface of that quickening ache, seeing daylight distorted and shiny from a long way away.

Sometimes she vomited. The vomiting frightened her. She preferred the fishhook.

Michael sat on the bus willing every stop to be a massive alighting of slow-moving people with heavy packages or children in bulky, difficult-to-maneuver prams. When the bus lumbered past a stop without crawling to a halt to accommodate time-consuming passengers, Michael found himself panicking. His self-control had been fraying for weeks, and delaying his arrival at Rose's was the only thing preventing that last thread from being pulled right down to the quick of his guts.

Rose had called while he was in his physics exam. They weren't allowed to have phones on them during exams and even though there was no frisking at the door, Michael had tucked his into his sock. He ignored it for as long as possible, but eventually the consistent vibrating against his malleolus began to register in his teeth. He slapped his unfinished paper onto the supervisor's desk and walked out. When he checked his phone there were five missed calls from Rose and a text message.

Come quick.

Rose straddled a chair in her bedroom and rocked back and forth. Her room was so hot. She had pulled the chair under the air-conditioning duct but the draft fell on her in a moist film. Her mouth felt dry and her lungs felt wet. She remembered her mother saying the air conditioner didn't work well in the humidity.

She leaned over the back of the chair and turned on the electric fan as well. Her forehead prickled as it dried out in the warm blast from the blades. She began to hum to herself — a rhythmic close-lipped chant that was caught by the fan and thrown back at her in a distorted tremble.

Crying, she reached for her phone to call Michael again but accidentally dropped it on the floor.

It started before the sun came up. Initially it wasn't too bad. Rose ignored it as best she could. When her mother left for work, Rose took a handful of painkillers she found secreted in her father's bedside table. She pinched the half-empty packet of cigarettes she found in there too.

But as the heat of the day began bleaching the small patch of sky visible from her bedroom window, Rose was gripped with it. The earth tilted, the poles shifted, and the sudden realization of what was happening to her hit her with agonizing loneliness.

Michael wasn't here. He hadn't called back. The only thing protecting Rose's sanity against her fear, in that moment, was the sensational shock of feeling, as if her body were turning inside out.

She had to get up to be sick again. She made it to the bathroom, holding onto the hall walls. She had nothing left to throw up and so dry-retched in convulsive spasms until the pressure in her bowel made it clear she needed to use the toilet.

The sensation was powerful and invigorating. Rose sat and strained and waited for the relief.

It was the only time she cried out.

When Michael arrived he couldn't find her at first and he thought, *Someone must have come home and found her and it's over now and I can fall down.*

Then he noticed a smudge of blood on the hall wall.

He found Rose in the bathroom, sitting on a towel and leaning up against the bath. She was smiling and brushing her hair.

The smell hit him at the same time, metal and ammonia. It made his tongue stick to the roof of his mouth. There was blood on the toilet seat and on the towel beneath Rose. All over her hands too.

He walked slowly forward and reached down to take the hairbrush out of Rose's grip.

He caught her wrist mid-brushstroke and said, "You're getting blood in your hair."

Rose stopped brushing and let go. The brush hung there on the side of her head, trapped in a wad of coagulated locks. Michael squatted down on his haunches and peeled Rose's hair away, then dropped the hairbrush in the bath. He touched the side of her face, which was hot and wet and swollen from crying.

Rose smiled again and said, "It went away."

Michael stood, but not straight up. He found that he had to drop back down to his knees for a moment and then use one knee to hoist himself upright.

He walked to the bathroom sink and tipped all the tooth-brushes out of the cup onto the vanity. Three people lived here but there were four toothbrushes. Why were there four toothbrushes? His own mother used a toothbrush to clean the tile grout in the shower, but she kept the cleaning tooth-brush well away from the ones that went inside people's mouths.

He quickly rinsed the cup and then filled it with water. He poured the water over Rose's hands and then wiped them off with one corner of the towel she was sitting on.

He filled the cup again and handed it to Rose.

He lifted it to her lips and said, "Drink this."

Michael walked over to the toilet and looked. His mouth quivered with a rush of saliva. Barbs of perspiration stung his pores. He concentrated on his breathing, dropped the lid and began to clean up.

It wasn't as big a job as Michael had first thought. Two rolls of paper towels and a bottle of spray bleach conveniently stored in the cupboard underneath the sink. He stripped down to his underwear and put on a pair of disposable surgical gloves — Rose had a box of them in the laundry that she used when she colored her hair. She said the gloves that came with the box of color were too loose. Twice he pulled the gloves off, carefully sliding them inside out, and put on a fresh pair.

Eventually he had to ease Rose up off the floor. The bloody towel she was sitting on stuck to her bottom. He peeled it off and helped Rose lift her T-shirt over her head. Then he got warm water running in the shower and helped her step into the recess. He squirted shampoo into her hand but she looked so confused that he stepped in with her and quickly washed her hair.

When he was helping her dry off, he noticed the bright dribble on the inside of her thigh. He left her holding a towel scrunched up under her chin and when he returned helped her step into a pair of knickers lined with a sanitary pad the size of a surfboard.

Michael was grateful for Rose's vacant compliance throughout the process. If she had been hysterical he didn't think he would have been capable of this shocking efficiency. And it was shocking. His every movement seemed to have a cerebral echo, as if it took his brain several seconds to register what his body was doing. He would begin to feel revulsion and fear, but too late. *That moment has passed and I am now performing the next frightening, revolting task which I won't register until I'm onto the one after that.*

It was keeping one step ahead of the rabid dog, and the rhythm of it kept him focused and wired.

Rose wandered into her bedroom and curled up on the bed. She tried to close her eyes but it felt too much like closing fingers around shattered glass. So she chose a point across the room and stared at it until she imagined she was a cat, and a sympathetic inner eyelid fluttered down to ease out the light.

When Michael walked in, dropping a large garbage bag in the hallway first, and found Rose wide-eyed and unmoving, it crossed his mind that she might have bled to death.

The thought made him momentarily angry so he said, "Knock it off, Rose. You're scaring the shit … out of me."

He didn't mean for his voice to get caught, but it did. He was high-pitched and shaky.

Then Rose sat up, a smooth movement, and said, "Bring it to me."

Michael had no hesitation with his response.

"No," he said matter-of-factly.

Rose looked at him then and blinked slowly.

"Yes," she said.

"I'll get rid of it," Michael said.

"It must be buried," Rose said, in a tone one might use with a small child who should know better.

We're almost there, we're almost there, Michael kept chanting to himself.

Rose continued to look at him as if appalled by a bad joke.

"We're almost there," he said out loud.

"It *must* be buried," Rose said again.

21

They waited until it was dark. Rose's mother had left a message on Rose's phone. Michael listened to it. She was going out with the girls after sculpture class and could Rose heat up some leftovers for dinner? She might be late.

Michael was pleased with the message. He listened to it twice. The events of the afternoon had swaddled him so tightly that it was a relief to hear that sculpture class was still going on and people were meeting after sculpture class, because it meant that other normal things were still going on outside of themselves.

They were almost there.

So they waited for dark. Michael wanted to go alone but Rose hadn't let go of it all afternoon. He considered wrenching it from her grip and just taking off, but in the end reckoned she had had enough wrenched from her body for one day. They didn't speak very much while they waited.

The dark finally crept across Rose's bedroom. Their eyes adjusted so incrementally that they didn't turn on a light but rather sat opposite one another just watching each other darken, Michael looking at Rose's silhouette, Rose looking at the tiny gray thing in her arms.

When Michael did switch a light on, he chose the hall light which set a yellowish pool across the bedroom threshold but did not come too close to Rose.

She said it was the perfect place. She had said it earlier in the day and she said it again as they walked down the street towards the large stretch of bushland that had swallowed an entire grown-up woman. Without a trace.

Rose chatted about the convenience and safety of it with the same nonchalance she exhibited with any other small talk. Michael carried the gym bag. He had convinced Rose with surprisingly little difficulty that they should put it in the gym bag to transport it because it was protected that way.

Michael counted the streetlights as they walked beneath them, feeling the light crawl across him, feeling exposed and vulnerable. Rose said they reminded her of the spotlights when she was on stage.

After the fifth streetlight, just before they entered the sphere of its smolder, Michael took Rose's hand and veered off into the scrub.

He led her reticently, saying, "Careful now, careful," until they were far enough into the undergrowth to use his phone screen as a torch without them being seen.

When Michael got home he noticed his fingernails were caked with black dirt. He rubbed his grubby hands on his jeans until they tingled with the friction, but nothing could hide the dirt packed under the nails. He dragged one nail through his teeth and then spat. He was going to need soap and water. He should have gone back to Rose's to clean himself up.

He had walked Rose home but didn't go in. Her mother's car was in the drive. He gave Rose very clear instructions before he left her. *Get straight into the shower; tell your mum you had dinner at my place; tell her you're really tired; go to bed; drink lots of water through the night.*

Michael was winging that last one but he was frightened by the amount of blood there had been and he knew blood loss required fluid replacement. He made her repeat the instructions back to him.

Rose had become very quiet on the walk home from the swallowing bush. It was as if something of her had been consumed there too, never to be seen again.

He watched her until she opened her front door. Then he doubled back and disposed of the towel in the dumpster.

It wasn't until Michael was standing at his own front door that he realized he had missed dinner without calling. He pulled his phone from his pocket.

Three missed calls from home. He'd left it on vibrate.

His mother was doing the dishes. His father was in front of the television.

Michael walked deliberately, briskly, to the bathroom.

The door was locked. He heard his father getting up, heard him making his way through the kitchen, heard a brief muffled exchange between his parents, worked the bathroom door handle frantically, shouldered the door a bit, palm-slapped it, heard his father behind him — and the door opened.

"Drugs?" Tim asked, standing before Michael completely naked. Tim reached behind Michael and locked the door. He quickly adjusted the egg timer to allow himself a further two minutes before stepping back into the running shower.

The door was thumped once.

"Drugs?" Tim asked again, slapping the shower curtain closed.

"No, thank you," Michael replied, sitting on the toilet lid.

It occurred to him this was the second bathroom he'd been in today that made him feel sick.

"Very funny. Bit of advice. Don't know what you're into or what's been happening but you're drawing a lot of attention from Mein Führer, mein friend."

Michael slowly stood and filled his hands with handwash from the pump pack on the edge of the bathroom sink. He massaged it into his skin slowly before turning on the water. The thick creamy soap blackened with grit and soil before slithering down the drain like a living thing.

Tim wrenched the shower curtain back and said, "Will you turn the fucking tap off while I'm in here?"

But Michael didn't. He was leaning on the edge of the sink, water still running, smears of dark dirt dappling the basin. He was crying.

Tim stepped out of the shower, water still running, and took Michael by the shoulders.

Before he could say anything, Michael fell into his brother's wet chest and sobbed.

22

Michael had never been a crier. In a house where self-expression of any kind was disapproved of, crying was an unusual event. Sometimes Michael would see his mother cry and it looked both painful and enjoyable at the same time. When he was very young he had cried when he was hurt or frustrated. His father would take his hand at these times and squeeze it until Michael felt that every bone was being crushed. The grip was always tender to begin with and then Michael would feel his thumb knuckle crack like a popgun.

Gradually that crying reflex was trained out of him. Instead he became quietly and unobtrusively self-soothing.

Now, as he gripped his brother and sobbed, he felt conflicted and guilty. He was even making noise with his crying. Big, gulping, howler-monkey swigs of air followed by piercing moans that made Tim hold him tighter and say things like, "Shhh!" and "They'll hear you!"

He cried for quite a while. Then he stopped as suddenly as he'd begun and dropped to the floor.

Tim stood over his brother for a few seconds, naked and in shock, before grabbing a couple of towels. He put the first one around Michael's shoulders and the second around his own waist.

They were both startled by thumping on the bathroom door, followed by the egg timer shrieking.

Tim quickly turned off the shower.

"What's going on in there?" Their father. "Someone better answer me."

"Out in a minute," Tim called. Then to Michael, "*What happened?*"

Michael looked at Tim blankly, a torrent of sensation burning under his skin.

"You're filthy. Is this blood?" Tim rubbed at the spots on Michael's sleeve. "Is this your blood?" He began feeling up and down his brother's arms. "Are you hurt? Did someone get hurt?"

Michael couldn't answer.

Tim squatted down and began removing Michael's shoes and socks. He gingerly coaxed Michael to his feet, pulled his shirt over his head and then began peeling off his jeans. Michael's knees were caked in dirt, hard with it in places. Michael instinctively placed his hands on Tim's shoulders in order to step out of each leg.

Tim started the shower then, and once Michael was under the running water, Tim pulled the shower curtain closed before saying, "Do you want to tell me what happened?"

And Michael did. He fixed his eyes on the tile grout, his retinas pulling together the edges of the small diamonds that created the mosaic wall. He stared, unflinching, as he talked, so that his vision swam, and the world threatened to turn inside out.

Then he dragged his focus to the showerhead, the taps, his hands held out in front of him as if in supplication, feeling his optic muscles protest as he clicked through changes in depth of field. He talked, finding it harder and harder to re-establish visual acuity.

Perhaps he was just tired. It had been a long day. The bathtub beneath him was white and curvaceous as the belly of a whale, the shower curtain rolling towards him like a comber about to fill his nostrils. He could taste it now, the bitter smack of seawater sweeping into his nose and mouth, but it was only his tears again, which baffled him.

He talked as if no one were listening, and he couldn't stop talking, couldn't believe the rush the relief alone gave him, just to say it out loud.

But something else happened as he talked too. All those preceding months of fear began to metastasize until he was shaking with the reality of what he had done. What they had done.

He paused, stopped talking for just a moment in order to lean against those small diamonds and breathe.

That's when Tim's hand appeared around the edge of the shower curtain and turned off the water.

They stood quietly on either side for a moment. Then Michael reached forward and eased the shower curtain back, the rings *clack, clack, clacking* against one another, a sound a bird might make.

Tim was sitting on the toilet lid staring at the shower curtain then staring at Michael as he was revealed.

The sudden rattling of the bathroom door handle shocked them both back into immediate reality.

"Out of there now," their father hollered, palm slapping the doorframe. "Michael, I want to talk to you."

Neither Michael nor Tim answered. It suddenly seemed very unimportant that their father was cross, ranting, waiting.

Michael said, "I'm so hungry."

Tim looked at him incredulously, then said, "Where did you …"

"In that bit of bush near her place. What am I going to do?"

Tim couldn't quite hold onto everything Michael had told him. He battled disbelief, all the while being sure of Michael's veracity.

Tim thought fast. What was there to do now? Hadn't it all been done? And wasn't he now, in Michael's telling of it, an accessory after the fact if he maintained the secret too?

He wondered why he wasn't angry. He waited, but anger never hit. Michael's face was frozen with a rime of desperation as tangible as the towel he now gripped under his chin.

Tim said, "You do nothing. You haven't really done anything anyway. Just cleaned up, right?"

Michael didn't answer.

Tim snapped his fingers a couple of times in Michael's face. *"Right?"*

"I suppose."

"Right. *She* hid it, *she* did it. You just got rid of it."

Michael stepped out of the shower and started to dry off,

started to feel, for the first time in months, a sort of release.

Tim continued, "You have to stop seeing her. Don't break up with her now. Just cool it, slowly. See her less and less. Put some distance there. Then put a lot of distance there."

"I love her," Michael said.

"Yeah, well, I've loved every girl I slept with … for a while. If you tell anyone now, you're screwed. And if the shit ever does hit the fan, you need to be telling your side away from her. You didn't even know she was knocked-up, right? You thought she was sleeping around. You didn't know what she was going to ask you to do when you went over there."

Tim was talking fast now, feeling Michael's escape from this glide into place like a bolt lock sliding home.

"You don't tell anyone. You don't talk about it with her. You forget about it. You haven't really done anything wrong. She has. You're not responsible for her choices. Do you get it?"

"I can't stop thinking about it."

"Well, think about this instead. If you tell, your life is over. Be smart."

Tim realized he was gripping Michael by the upper arms.

He scooped up Michael's dirty clothes and shoes from the bathroom floor and moved to the door.

"I'll take care of these," he said. "And we'll never talk about it again either."

Tim eased the bathroom door open just a crack, antici- pating being met by a trebuchet of his father's displeasure.

He was surprised and relieved to find the hallway clear. Harold had retreated, temporarily at least.

Michael looked at himself in the mirror after Tim left.

Although his eyes were a bit swollen and he was pale, he didn't look any different. He hadn't really looked at himself for weeks. Nothing showed. Not a thing.

He was so hungry.

23

Rose walked quietly into the house. The front door was sticky and the rubbing of door against frame was usually concluded with a short sharp thud. She pushed with her shoulder, anchoring the door's movement with gentle reverse pressure on the door handle. When it finally landed flush she didn't turn the deadlock. It always made a clack that echoed and she wasn't ready to announce herself.

It wasn't until Rose was in her bedroom that her mother called out to her. Just the usual greeting and the usual assumption about lateness.

"You been to Michael's for dinner?"

From the kitchen. Her mother was in the kitchen.

Rose called out, "Yes!" A small pause, then, "I'm going to shower!"

As soon as Rose entered the bathroom, the smell and taste of bleach stung her. Every sense was suddenly, vibrantly alive. Her skin crackled with it.

She quickly opened the bathroom window and lit the scented candles her mother kept on the ledge at the end of the bath. She started the shower running and let the steam build up, then punched holes in it with shots of the lemon verbena flyspray her mother kept under the sink because she couldn't stand the daddy longlegs that always seemed to find their way into the bathtub.

Then Rose undressed and got into the shower. She slid down the wall and sat in the bottom of the recess feeling the stench of bleach draining away. She sat there for a long time.

When she finally emerged from the bathroom, her mother was standing on the other side of the door.

"Mum!" Rose snapped back into herself with the fright of her mother's unexpected proximity.

"Did you clean the bathroom today?"

"What?"

"Did you clean the bathroom today." Statement this time, rather than question.

"No, I ..."

Rose was suddenly angered by the challenge. Except her mother didn't look at all challenging. She just looked sad.

Rose considered saying it then, saying it into her mother's sad face so redolent of a fear she had no right to feel.

Rose imagined the words coming out, imagined those words smelling of suspicious bleach and insect poison. *Michael cleaned the bathroom because I bled in there and then we buried it.*

But she couldn't do it. Rose had worked so hard at this and now, finally, everything could go back to normal. The time for telling was past.

So she said yes.

She pushed past her mother and headed down the hall to her room.

As she shut the door she heard her mother call after her, "Don't use so much bleach next time."

It wasn't until Rose was back in her room, leaning against the closed door, that she noticed the gym bag on the end of her bed. She didn't even remember carrying it in with her. She couldn't remember when Michael had given it to her. She didn't know why he hadn't taken it with him and gotten rid of it.

Rose took the bag and shoved it under her bed, against the wall.

It was the last thing she was capable of doing. Her limbs were shaking. She was incredibly thirsty. She remembered Michael telling her to drink lots of water but all she wanted to do was sleep.

As she went to lie down on the bed she noticed a dark, slightly tacky stain on the sheet and knew it would have seeped through to the mattress beneath. Rose fingered it a little. It was still damp. She lay on top of it, feeling its slight coolness crawl onto her bare thigh, imagining her own weight pushing it farther and farther into the mattress until it was undetectable.

Michael's phone screen cast an arc of light bigger and brighter than anything Rose had ever seen before. He was swinging it wildly from tree to tree and she had trouble keeping up. She stumbled several times and tried to call out to him to slow down, to stop, but her voice wouldn't carry a sound and he ran on, oblivious. The trees were ghost-ashen and full of uneasy movement. Every flash of light that scoured them was like an eager eye in a game of statues. Rose knew each tree used its moment of darkness to skulk towards her, and she understood now that Michael was protecting her with his light, keeping the onslaught back with every sweep of illumination. So she struggled on, following his pallid luminescence, feeling colder and colder the deeper and farther they went.

And before she knew it, she was standing in that light on the edge of a deep chasm, her bare feet bruised and bloodied, balancing precariously on the edge, her toes hooked into the soft dirt for purchase. And she had a full and terrible knowledge of how she had gotten there. Michael was digging this crater in their sphere of light and then she was too — squeezing earth in her fingers, tossing the clods behind her to prevent the advance of the darkened trees.

Michael looked up at her and said, "We're almost there," and she knew she had to jump into the hole they had prepared, but it was very deep and she was frightened.

She hesitated only a moment and then stepped forward into airlessness. She couldn't fill her lungs, and she was falling and falling and when she felt the first *thunk* of backfill, cold against her dank skin, she woke up with a scream in her throat and her mouth feeling as if it was full of dirt.

Rose wasn't sure if she had made any noise. She was sitting upright, her arms outstretched behind her, elbows locked.

It took her some time to orient herself, to crawl out of the dream. Her mouth was parched and she felt sogginess between her legs.

How long had she been sleeping? Had she really slept?

With effort, Rose managed to ease her arms out of the rigor mortis of nightmare and reach across to turn on her light.

She grabbed her phone: 3:00 a.m. There was a calendar alert on the screen: Lit Exam Today 10:00 am.

Rose knew she had to get up to go to the toilet, but her phone listed in and out of focus, a watery mirage, and the floor seemed a long way away. So thirsty.

There was an old can of Red Bull on the night stand. She leaned across and managed to pincer it with thumb and forefinger. When she lifted it to her mouth the taste of her dream rushed to the back of her throat, along with an old, wet cigarette filter.

Rose spat and coughed until she retched.

She didn't know what made her do it. She had no clear recollection of sliding her phone screen to that particular contact.

But suddenly there was the voice on the other end, tinny and feeble with sleep.

Rose began to cry when she heard it.

"Hello? Hello? Jesus Christ, what fucking time is it?"

Rose couldn't respond. She listened to the muted sounds of movement, imagining Liv struggling with bed covers, trying to sit up, leaning on that dodgy elbow she dislocated playing hockey in primary school. They had to call an ambulance and everything.

Rose remembered Liv couldn't feel her hand when it happened. She had been terrified by that lack of feeling.

Then, "Rose? Rosie?"

Rose didn't remember falling asleep.

24

Liv walked into Rose's bedroom and closed the door behind her. Rose was sitting in her underwear on the edge of her bed.

"So, your mum says I'm to make sure you get moving because you have an exam today. She's on her way to work. Passed her in the driveway. She thinks you might not be feeling well. Are you feeling unwell, Rose? I hope so. I'd like you to be feeling unwell on an exam day. Is that why you called me last night? Oh, excuse me, *this morning*? At three fucking *a.m.*?"

Liv had spent the previous four hours getting angry. The anger came fast. She hadn't heard from Rose in months and resented the fact that the minute Rose woke her with a phone call she involuntarily reverted to the two emotions she had spent those months rejecting: worry and love. She was angry that having been thrown away she found herself still clinging to remnants of someone she hardly even recognized anymore.

"Liv? Can you get me a drink of water, please?"

"It stinks in here. And it's so fucking dark."

Liv strode to the window and yanked the blind so hard it retracted with the speed and clatter of a slot machine.

She looked down at Rose.

Then she said, "Oh fuck."

Rose was the color of newspaper. She was shaking. Her hands rested on her knees, palms up, fingers slightly crooked. There was blood on them.

Liv bolted to the kitchen and grabbed a bottle of water from the fridge. She ran back so fast she skidded on the hall rug and slammed her shoulder into the wall.

Rose didn't respond to the water Liv held in front of her. She seemed to be looking at it but when Liv knelt down she realized Rose's eyes were rolled ever-so-slightly back in her head.

Liv pressed the bottle to Rose's lips and tipped. She couldn't tell how much went in Rose's mouth. A lot spilled down her chest but she was sure she saw a swallow.

She tipped again and this time Rose swallowed more.

"I've been thirsty," Rose said, and then slowly tilted forward until she slid to her knees on the floor, landing with the grace of a cat on Liv's chest.

"Oh fuck."

Liv eased Rose onto the floor and grabbed her phone. It slipped out of her grasp. She realized her own hands were bloodied and quickly wiped them on the edge of Rose's bed before making the call.

"Oh fuck, oh fuck ..."

"Hello?"

"... oh fuck, oh fuck ... Mum?"

"Livvie? Is that you?"

"Please come. Please come to Rose's. Oh fuck, Mum."

"Jesus, baby. I'm still in bed. What's going on?"

"Please come to Rose's, Mum. She ... she ..."

"Tell me what's wrong. Now!"

"I just need you."

"On my way."

When Liv's mother pulled into the driveway, Liv was waiting for her on the front steps. She had been running back and forth between Rose's bedroom and the front steps of the house for the past twenty minutes.

She imagined her action — some action, any action — could both speed up time and create a bubble of it that could never be pricked. To keep moving in this immediate moment became more and more senseless and more and more essential. So she ran.

And then she ran to the door of her mother's car, yanked it open and began pulling on her mother's clothes before the seatbelt was even disengaged.

"Jesus Christ, is that your blood?"

"Oh fuck, oh fuck, Mum."

"Is that your blood?"

It was only then that Liv realized she had blood on her clothes.

"No." Liv grappled at her mother, incapable of standing still. "No. Rose's."

Once inside, Liv's mother brought a kind of steely efficiency to the situation that was unrecognizable to Liv. And that's what she called it. A situation.

She said, "This is quite a situation, this is *quite* a situation," with a droll curl of her mouth and cool, quick-moving hands that calmed both girls almost immediately. She issued instructions without asking too many questions.

Together Liv and her mother successfully maneuvered Rose into the front seat of the car, Liv's mother shoving a rolled-up towel between Rose's legs before slamming the door and saying, "Let's get this situation off the boil, shall we?"

Liv was about to climb into the back seat when her mother grabbed her upper arm and said, "Where's the baby?"

Liv stared at her mother blankly. That bubble of time precariously held aloft by all of the preceding madness gently touched down and burst like a squeezed fig.

"Don't know," she responded.

"You stay here," her mother ordered. "Clean yourself up. Take those clothes off and get into something of Rose's. Make yourself a cup of tea. You look like shit."

She opened her car door and was about to climb in when she turned and added, "Where's her mother?"

Liv waited for five hours and while she waited, while she hovered somewhere between the fear and weariness that was peculiar to waiting for what you thought would be bad news, she cleaned. She cleaned Rose's bedroom floor until her hands were scalded by hot water. She washed the bed frame and the walls where she found bloody handprints. She felt an overwhelming need to get rid of the smell.

Blood didn't bother her. She had peeled bloodied shirts off her mother before, while gently compressing the nose hemorrhages that seemed to be the exit strategy of most of her mum's boyfriends.

She stuffed everything that needed to be washed into the corner of the laundry behind the door. And then she waited some more.

She thought about calling Michael but she had deleted his number from her phone. She thought about how Rose's skin had been the texture of a ghost gum, how her eyes had rolled in her head. Liv thought about how she had stayed out of it and how she should never have punished Rose's rejection of her by staying out of it until she was washing blood off the floorboards.

Her mother returned just after midday.

"Rose had an emergency D and C. She had a partially retained placenta and was in hypovolemic shock," she said heavily.

"Did you take her to a hospital?" Liv asked. She didn't know what hypovolemic shock was.

"No," her mother replied. "I performed the procedure myself and she's now in the boot of our car. Jesus!" She dropped into a chair and closed her eyes. "You did the right thing, Liv."

Liv wasn't sure exactly what she had done right.

"Okay," she replied. "I did the right thing by staying out of it?"

"Yes, by staying out of it and getting back in when you did."

Liv wasn't sure about that but her mother lived her life by staying out of things. She said you didn't get hurt that way. She said if you wanted people to mind their own business then you minded your own first.

Liv asked, "Is she coming home now?"

It sounded like a ridiculous thing to ask. Would her mother have taken Rose to the hospital and then left her to get a bus home?

As soon as Liv thought about it, she realized it was a distinct possibility.

"No. She'll be in the hospital overnight. Intravenous fluids."

Then it happened. That sudden dissipation of stress hormones so necessary to making any trauma look like *just a situation* for as long as it took to survive it.

Liv began to cry.

"You can stop that now," her mother said, standing up and pulling Liv to her feet by the shoulders. "You really can, Livvie. It's all okay. Now let's go home. I gave the hospital her mum's name but I'm sure a courtesy call to old crazy Violet is the etiquette here."

25

Rose told the doctors she had miscarried and accidentally flushed the bits that came out down the toilet. Now her mother sat beside the hospital bed, her hand barely resting on top of her daughter's.

Violet had no frame of reference for this so she simply sat, quietly looking down at the blanket stretched over Rose's slightly crooked knees, her head snapping up at the sound of every passerby, watching for those who slowed by the ward door, watching for those who might know. A furtive surveillance, avoiding eyes.

Rose looked at her mother long enough to understand that her gaze would not be returned. So she watched the shadow from the banksia tree outside the window rattle about on the slick linoleum tile beneath her mother's chair. Sometimes in high wind the tree would rock forward just enough to scrape against the window like Catherine Earnshaw.

That's what Rose imagined, anyway. That a ghost would have a lithe touch and sound like nature at the window.

Violet lived a life that had diminished her to the point of

glances. No real eye contact. Just a hooded flash of white at whatever confronted her. Rose wondered if self-preservation was at the root of her mother's need to avoid people's eyes and the reason she must now have felt so personally affronted by the bold pain she saw in Rose's.

Rose knew that if her mother really looked at her now she would see way beyond the cat's cradle of carefully woven facade Rose clung to.

But she didn't. Violet studied the hospital blanket and Rose stared at the banksia's shadow until her eyes felt like fat furry grapes that could be popped with a blink.

"Mum?" Rose's voice quivered a little.

"Had to hear about it from strangers," Violet said quietly.

"Mum, I'm scared."

"Do you know how that makes me look?"

Rose closed her eyes and listened to the blood in her ears until everything else sounded a long way away.

She heard her mother's voice, registering the slight chirrup returning to her tone as she said, "Well, it's all over now. No one need ever know. We'll speak to the school. I'm sure there is a contingency in place for students who miss exams due to illness. We'll say you were admitted to hospital for exhaustion ... or food poisoning. You don't have to worry about it. You just get well. Did I tell you your father's on his way home? He was able to get a flight straight away. Everyone was so understanding when they heard his daughter was sick in hospital. Don't you worry about ..."

Violet's voice drifted away down voluminous hospital corridors, winged and optimistic.

When Rose opened her eyes, her mother was talking animatedly at the hospital blanket.

Back at home, on bed rest, iron supplements and cigarettes, Rose grew to understand just how invested her mother was in the exhaustion/food poisoning story. Rather than settle quietly and privately into her daughter's recovery, Violet proactively disseminated news on the phone regarding the speed with which her daughter's illness came on, the unfortunate timing of it, the understanding and support provided by the school in the case of someone as high-achieving as Rose falling ill during exams, and the rapidity of Rose's recovery which was, after all, a testament to her strength and commitment to her future.

The church rallied behind Violet and there were even flowers from the youth group leader, which Violet placed in Rose's room with the kind of mawkish flourish usually reserved for new mothers.

Rose grew angry at her mother for not recognizing the irony. Violet told Rose not to be ungrateful and to finish her dinner.

Meals were delivered to Rose in bed, on a tray. Her father would occasionally pop his head in the door and ask after "his girl" and tell her she looked much better, and Rose began to wonder whether her father was actually given the same story as the youth group leader.

Rose cut a small square out of the corner of her bedroom flyscreen with nail scissors and used the hole to poke her still-smoldering butts out into the garden bed below her window. At night, she dreamed of the fallen leaves beneath catching fire, and the fire spreading and taking the house and her away in tiny flesh-smelling sparks, like living fireworks, while her mother and father and the youth group leader watched and waved from below.

Michael didn't visit. Rose wondered if he had been told he couldn't.

Liv came and sat on Rose's bed. She immediately noticed the new mattress. Felt the brittle sigh of a plastic mattress protector as she sank onto it. Smelled the stale cigarette smoke and remnants of cleaning fluid. Heard Violet knock and wait for permission to enter the room before easing the door open with a hesitance that suggested a fear of what she might see or smell. Noticed the carefully staged mood of the recovery and the unspoken expectation to participate in the delusion that Rose was a victim of something far outside her own control.

"In the nineteenth century," Liv said, "ladies with the Romantic Disease would lie in state in sanatoriums built at high altitude, surrounded by flowers and deferential staff wearing crisp white." She looked from side to side. "There's a whiff of that here, Rosie. Do you feel your weakened state has made you more spiritually aware?"

Rose managed a brief but genuine smile.

"I don't feel anything much, really," she replied. "Relief that it's over. Have you seen Michael?"

"Yeah," Liv said.

"Does he know I'm sick?"

"Don't know what he knows," Liv said.

She had seen Michael at school recently when they sat

the same exam. She didn't approach him, even though she wanted to. She looked at him and he flicked his eyes in her direction several times, but they didn't speak. Throughout the exam, he kept leaning down and touching his ankle with a bizarre tic-like repetition. Liv thought he probably had notes in his sock.

"Mum took my phone off me," Rose said.

"I know. I called you and she answered."

"She talked to your mum."

"I know that too," Liv said. "I think that's the only reason I'm allowed in to see you. She probably thinks it's safer having me on the inside."

Liv paused, wondering how to get where she wanted to go. Her mum had told her not to ask. Her mum had told her to mind her own business.

"Rose," she began. "Rosie, what happened? Where is it?"

Rose knew that Liv would understand. Rose felt the words, the explanation, the night that felt like a story that had happened to someone else rise in her like her dream fireworks.

But, as always, since the moment in the hospital when her mother had found her too abhorrent to look at, Rose's craving to spit out the facts was suddenly choked. Instead she felt the foulness of the truth sit in her mouth like a wad of over-chewed gum.

So she said, "It was a terrible miscarriage, Liv. I didn't realize what was going on at first." Rose began to cry. "It hurt badly, and then it was over, and I flushed it away. I'm so glad you were here for me, and as soon as I'm over this stomach flu, I know I'll feel better." She paused before saying, "I know I'll get better."

Liv held Rose's hand feeling appalled. There was obviously no way to ever get where she wanted to go in this conversation because Rose herself had already been sucked into a survival lie that was impenetrable.

Liv leaned forward and kissed Rose on the cheek.

"I have to go, but I'll be back tomorrow."

"I love you, Livvie."

"I love you too, Rosie."

As Liv pulled away and stood up, she noticed Rose's breasts were leaking.

26

During the next week a frail normality returned. The sort of normality based on routine and the embrace of the familiar. There was a tacit understanding that Rose's exhaustion/food poisoning, once passed, would not be alluded to again.

Rose privately sat the exams she had missed by special arrangement with the school, and felt confident and satisfied upon their completion. Rose and Liv were as close as they had ever been, as if the preceding months of non-communication had never occurred. Rose's father left for work again, leaving his girls behind for another few weeks of agreeable together time. And Rose's mother joined a book club started by the president of the ladies' auxiliary at church, the first book selection of which was *The Scarlet Letter* by Hawthorne.

One thing did not return to normal, however. Rose and Michael still hadn't spoken to each other since it happened. They somehow — instinctively rather than intentionally — avoided each other.

Rose had developed a kind of emotional catatonia that scared Michael. She was always with that Liv and that scared him too. She seemed disturbingly vacant and had developed a shuffle when she walked.

Once when Michael was approaching her on the street she stopped and gazed at him with a tiny but friendly frown, as if she was suddenly confronted by someone she knew a long time ago and was having trouble putting a name to the face.

Michael turned and walked away because looking at her left him winded.

With final exams over, the long wait for scores and the search for summer jobs began. They were all on the cusp of applying for their futures, as if the future were an impassable gateway that required all manner of romancing and coercing to allow the next generation through.

Michael understood that his future would not simply come to him. The days would not open up, filled with promise and prospect. He must pry open his own life as if it were a tight fist hiding a shiny penny.

But, truth told, he had very little fight left in him.

His father said nothing when Michael stopped accompanying the family to church. At least, he said nothing to Michael. He no longer asked after Michael's day at the dinner table. He no longer offered to take Michael out for a drive.

It was the withholding dance. A sly, punitive conscience-tickle that would usually have motivated Michael to seek out his father's approval and re-engagement with more vigor.

But Michael didn't. His impetus rusted to a halt in the face of a silent aggression he believed he deserved.

His family had been his center. Without that firmness, his circle was not just.

Michael heard about the party from Ryan and Sam. Everyone was going. It was the sort of event that Michael would previously have talked to his father about. His father would have dropped him off and picked him up afterwards. His father would have spoken to the parents of the host and, if the party was unsupervised, permission to attend would have been denied.

Michael told his mother he was going to a movie with friends after dinner because he didn't want to worry her and he wanted her to have something to tell his father when his father asked her where Michael was. She kissed him on the cheek and told him to have a good time.

They started drinking in the car. These were the friends he knew, the friends who would never ask what was wrong, who would never suspect his sullen silence to be anything other than the cultivation of maximum velocity drunkenness.

Michael sucked down every can handed to him — the tart, the syrupy, the astringent blasts of unknown brews that cleared his sinuses and heated his organs. He was not a drinker. He didn't even like the taste. But the pounding throb of the car sub in his spine and the mesmeric speed with which things standing still flew past his window, awakened something in Michael already forever altered and needing to be quieted: his conscience. The alcohol smacked his better judgment into silence. It was the first peace he had experienced in months.

By the time they arrived at the party, the neighbors had

already called the police once to complain about the noise and sound of breaking glass. He didn't know whose house it was. Several cars were parked on the front lawn, one of which had reversed into a concrete birdbath, knocking it over and taking out a taillight.

They made their way to the front door to find it locked. The flyscreen had been pried off and was lying, slightly buckled, on the verandah. One of the decorative leadlight panels in the door was smashed.

They followed the sound of music and reveling down the side of the house to the backyard.

Someone thrust a cup of something into Michael's hand as he made his way through the crowd. He tripped over a crying girl who was sitting on the ground leaning up against an esky. He was shouldered roughly and accidentally by someone who spilled the contents of their plastic cup over his arm.

Ryan and Sam had already peeled away from him to complete their own reconnaissance, so Michael found himself alone in the center of a cacophony of writhing blitheness that was the first thing louder than his own thoughts in days.

That's when he saw her. Liv. Leaning up against a tree near the back fence, her fingers hooked into the belt loops of some guy's jeans. This guy's hands all over her in a drunken frisk.

Michael didn't know why, but he walked straight over to her and said, "Is she here?"

Liv extricated herself from the muddle of limbs encircling her and stared at Michael in disbelief.

"Is who here?" she said.

"Rose."

"Hey, buddy," the frisker said impatiently. "Wait your turn."

"Of course she's not here," Liv replied. Then, "Are you drunk?"

"I thought she might be ... here. With you."

"We're busy," the frisker said.

"No, we're not," Liv said, pushing him away.

She looked down at the cup Michael was drinking from. There was a cigarette butt floating in it.

She slapped it out of his hand. The remnants of warm, grimy swill that had once been a beer splashed across the frisker's shirt.

He took a step back, arms extended and said, "Fucking bitch," before shoving Liv against the tree.

Michael took a swing at the frisker then, but failed to connect and fell face down onto the grass.

The fall seemed to take a long time. He watched the ground coming closer and closer, waited for impact, his throat burning with nausea. He stayed where he landed.

From his prone position, the undulating lawn looked like a foreign landscape as vast and complicated as any planet. The blades of grass were taller than trees. Michael imagined being a pinhead-sized visitor in a land of giants, ducking and weaving between smooth painted toenails that threatened to crush him.

There was one in front of him right now. Slightly chipped polish, a plaited gold toe ring.

Then a white knee descended like a moon inches from

his eyes, and he realized Liv was sitting on the grass next to him.

"We buried it, you know."

Liv leaned down closer and placed one cool palm on Michael's back. It reminded him of her hand on his chest that day in the park.

"What did you say?" she asked quietly.

"We buried it."

27

Liv drove Michael home. They didn't wait until the party ended. Those things never had a real ending anyway. Just a disinterested winding down once someone got arrested or the number of the unconscious exceeded that of the remaining drinkers.

As soon as Liv was able to coax Michael into an upright position, she loaded him into her mother's car and took him back to her place. She was going to take him back to his, but she didn't know if he'd be able to make it to his front door, let alone find his bedroom quietly to pass out.

Rose had told Liv about his parents. It didn't seem right to allow Michael to be found lying on the front doorstep in the morning covered in his own vomit, even though recent events did cause Liv to pause and consider the justice of leaving him in exactly that position. On the way home she had to stop on the side of the freeway for him to lean out of the car door and be sick.

Once home she dragged him inside, cursing a blue streak at Rose, him and herself. In the hallway outside her bedroom door, just a few steps from her bed, he slid down the wall like an avalanche. Liv knew there was no way she could halt the momentum of all that dead weight.

So she let go, stepped over him, pulled her dress up over her head and crawled into bed.

"Liv? Livvie!"

In the morning Liv was woken by the sound of her name being hollered from somewhere else in the house.

She sat up, checked her phone for messages, and then responded.

"Mum?"

"Yes. You want coffee, baby? Oh, and there's a boy in the hall."

Liv looked over the end of her bed and saw Michael in the exact position she had left him. He had just begun to stir.

"Yes, please. I know there's a boy in the hall," Liv called back.

"Have you checked it for a pulse?"

Michael was pulling himself into a sitting position. He leaned back against the hall wall and closed his eyes.

Liv's mum appeared then. She stepped over Michael's legs, sat on the edge of Liv's bed and handed her daughter a cup of coffee.

"Thanks, Mum."

"So," her mum said, looking directly at Michael.

"Hello. I'm really sorry about this. I don't know …"

Michael's tongue felt like a dead rodent. There was a blacksmith pounding red-hot metal behind his eyes. His jeans were damp with night sweat, and his shirt sported a large scab of dried vomit from mid-chest to waist.

Liv's mother stood before saying, "I'll get you something."

She stepped over his legs and strode back up the hall.

Liv sipped her coffee and watched Michael shifting uncomfortably on the floor.

He said, "I think I'm hungover."

"You think?"

"Aren't you?"

"No. I didn't drink last night."

Liv put her coffee down and propped some pillows against the wall at the end of her bed. Then she snapped her fingers and pointed to the nest she had created.

"Take your shirt off, then get up here."

Michael did as he was told. He pulled his shirt up over his head, then wiped his face with the only clean bit he could find. He held it in front of him, looking questioningly at Liv, who pointed to a plastic-lined wicker wastebasket next to a one-eyed rocking horse. Michael dropped his shirt in and then crawled on hands and knees across the bed until he was sitting against the pillows. The comfort was exhilarating.

Liv's mum walked back into the room with a cup of coffee in one hand and a water bottle in the other. She handed them to Michael and walked out.

"Do you remember last night?" Liv asked.

Michael took a swig of water and then began to sip the coffee.

He said, "Bits and pieces. I'm in a lot of trouble."

"I was going to take you back to yours, but this seemed easier. I'm not even a hundred percent sure which house on that street is yours. I might have left you on someone else's front doormat."

"No, I …"

Michael paused. He was lost. And for just a moment he enjoyed the sensation of the bereft vanishing of any rational thought or feeling.

Liv's mum stuck her head around the corner of the doorframe then and dropped some clothes on top of the rocking-horse saddle, saying to Michael, "Clean shirt, pants. Have a shower if you like. I have to go." Then to Liv, "Take care, baby girl."

Liv's mum scanned the room briefly, then quickly picked up the wicker wastebasket and took it with her.

Liv was worried that at any moment the bubble might burst. Just enough morning-after horror might be awakened by Michael's coffee to cause him to bolt, so she abandoned all subtlety and said, "You buried it."

Michael felt a sudden shift in the room. It was more than the hectic quiver of things in his line of vision that he knew to be motionless. He had been experiencing that since he first opened his eyes.

It was the realization that he was in the bedroom of someone he despised while not being able to remember why he despised her. It was the realization that at some time last night he had told Liv what they had done. Liv had brought him here rather than leave him in a stranger's backyard. Liv who had never told what she knew even though he had called her a slag.

Liv sat cross-legged up against her pillows drinking the coffee her mum had made.

"Thank you," Michael said.

"For what?"

"For letting me sleep on your floor."

Liv struggled with her next question. She had been combating Rose's denial, fearing it, submitting to it, for over a week. Liv had watched Rose slide down the rabbit hole, fearing her own perceptions were being dragged along for the ride.

Someone had to ask the question. Someone had to slap this denial upside the head.

With her mother's *stay out of it* clinging like teeth to her reason, Liv asked, "Was it a boy or a girl?"

Michael felt the smack of reality through his crawling nausea. It was too much. Until this moment he had coped in the way that people cope with big things. He had diminished it, justified it, avoided it and buried it. He had stayed away from Rose, watched her from a distance, watched her being diminished and buried herself.

He was still fighting the swarm of his own thoughts when Liv added, "Rose isn't dealing with this. I'm frightened for her."

Michael shimmied to the edge of the bed, sloshing his coffee onto his jeans and Liv's sheets. He skidded on a skin of his own vomit as he hit the hallway, then ran from the house, shirtless.

When he hit the pavement he realized he was still carrying the coffee cup. He threw it into someone's yard and kept running.

28

Rose's mother was hanging Christmas decorations when she said, "I think they found that woman."

Rose looked up and asked, "What woman?"

"You know. *That* woman," Rose's mother continued. "The one who went missing a couple of years ago. They suspected the husband, I think. Remember all that digging in the bush? I certainly do."

"Oh yeah, I remember that."

"Well, they're back down there again and this time there's crime-scene tape up. Guess I'll have to start using the other petrol station again."

Rose went to her room. She called Michael but he didn't answer. She didn't leave a message.

She looked at the time. Michael would be at dinner right now and he wasn't allowed to have his phone on him at the dinner table. After dinner he'd see the missed call and call her back. She was sure of it.

Rose waited. She felt peculiarly calm. Someone must have found it. Ludicrously, she hadn't even considered that a possibility.

He had. He fought her at every turn until after the deed was done. He didn't want to bury it. He cried doing it. He wanted to put it in the dumpster with the towel.

But Rose had insisted it needed a burial. His hands tugged at the dirt, pulling fistfuls of the black stuff aside in a deformed breaststroke while his body shook with hiccupy moans.

He watched her watching him, holding it. The deeper he dug, the farther away the hole looked.

She passed a large clot while he dug and had to lean against a tree to stop from fainting.

She smiled down at him and said, "This is the right thing to do," and in that moment she believed it.

Rose lay down on her bed, pulling her pillow up under her chin, and waited. Maybe she was worrying for nothing. Maybe they really had found that woman. That woman who walked out of her house and never returned. She would be just bones by now, Rose imagined.

Rose's mother had a cutlery set with bone handles. Rose wondered where someone would get the bones to make those handles and other bone things. She imagined there was a committee of bone collectors who went about scavenging dead things, waiting for the flesh to fall off so they could harvest the bones. Should be able to make a whole cutlery set out of this missing woman.

Rose's mother was particularly fond of her bone-handled cutlery set. It had once belonged to her own mother. She said they were well balanced and felt good in the hand. Rose was told that she would be given that cutlery set one day. It had great sentimental value and real bone was rare. Everything was plastic or stainless steel nowadays.

Rose could pass those bone handles down to her own children. The thought soothed her.

Rose was nodding off to sleep when her mother stuck her head in the bedroom door and said, "Rosie. They found a baby in the bush."

Rose pushed herself up onto one elbow and asked, "Are there any pieces missing in that cutlery set? You know, the one that was Grandma's with the bone handles?"

Her mother didn't respond.

Rose waited a moment. "Mum? Why are you crying?"

Michael wasn't at the dinner table. He was sitting in his room holding his phone when it rang. He almost answered it. He had just heard the evening news and was considering calling Rose when she called him. Dinner being late tonight, his father had the news on while Michael was setting the table.

That's when Michael heard it.

Police tonight are searching an area of bushland in the southern suburbs after discovering the remains of what appears to be a near-to-term female infant. The discovery was made this morning by a local man walking the area with his dogs. The man's attention was drawn to what has been described by police as a shallow grave, when his dogs began digging in the vicinity. A police spokesperson said no further information was available at this time. However, an autopsy is being performed. The death is being treated as suspicious.

So Michael sat in his bedroom considering calling Rose and then ignoring her call to him.

He didn't know what he would say to her anyway.

The truth was, Michael couldn't think about her or look at her without seeing the blood. He would drag her into focus with an effort that sprained his retinas and just when he thought her face would stay before him the way it used to, the edges of her would bleed out and darken until she was as crusted and virulent as the bloodied towel now festering in the dumpster behind the market.

Except the towel wouldn't be there anymore, would it? It would be long since buried under tonnes of other refuse at the landfill.

They should have thrown it away with the towel. People didn't walk their dogs through the landfill. And even if they did, no one was interested in what a dog sniffed in a landfill. People dumped dead cats in there, after all.

It didn't matter now. It had been found and there was nothing they could do about it. Nor did they have to. There was no way, Michael thought, that they could connect it with him.

Tim walked into Michael's bedroom and shut the door. Of all the things competing for cognitive brain space in that moment, the shutting of his bedroom door screamed the loudest.

"Open the door!" he hissed at Tim.

"I don't think so!" Tim riposted. He stood with his back pressed against the closed door. The hard, cool surface sent a kind of current into his muscle tissue as if he were leaning against their father's tangible displeasure.

Pressing up against all the possible repercussions of having a door closed against his father gave Tim a shot of perspective more piercing than a bullet.

He said, "You can't wait for them to come to you."

"Who?"

"The police!"

"Why would they come to me?" Michael asked.

Tim couldn't decide whether Michael was genuinely confused or diabolically stupid.

"They'll come to you because they'll work it out. You can't risk them tracking you down. The bigger this thing gets, the worse it's going to be when they do find you. Don't you get it? Now's the time. Get in first and tell your side. You have to protect yourself."

Protect yourself. The words had talons.

"Rose just called me," Michael said.

"Well, don't answer!"

Tim felt more and more frustrated. This wasn't just about protecting Michael anymore. This was about protecting himself. Could he trust Michael not to reveal that he had told him everything that had happened that very night? Could he even ask Michael to do that?

"Listen," Tim said, trying to keep the desperation out of his voice, "we work out exactly what you're going to say. You are remorseful, upset. You tried all along to get this girl to do the right thing but she wouldn't. You know you did the wrong thing by not coming forward sooner. But all you did, Michael, was dispose of the evidence of her crime. Okay?"

Michael watched his brother talking, heard the words, his burgeoning panic turning into a fat wet cud.

He said, "Let me think, let me think."

Tim let his head drop back against the door and groaned. Then he turned away and opened the bedroom door.

Standing on the threshold was their father, one hand on each doorjamb.

"Dinner's ready," was all he said.

29

"The Baby in the Bush" was front-page news, first in their immediate community and then farther and farther afield. Professionals from all kinds of medical and legal fields were weighing in on the discovery, and the commentary took on the grave agenda-laden authority of people so excited by the horror of it that soon the infant itself was hardly mentioned.

This small, abandoned thing was fast becoming a symbol for the collapse of societal standards and the degradation of the value of human life. Ministers and politicians seethed about the influence of violent video games, movies and music on the vulnerable youth of today. Assumptions were made that fast became printed copy and therefore recognized fact. A wound-up public would have something to rage about in bank and supermarket queues for weeks.

The crime-scene tape stayed up for three days. Small crowds gathered to watch the police in white jumpsuits moving like wraiths in and out of sight, at once hidden, then starkly exposed against the dark underbrush and conch-pale trees. There was a reverential solemnity to it all. There was talk of seasoned officers needing counseling, and locals began leaving flowers up against the streetlight on the corner.

Rose read and listened to the diatribe with curiosity and incredulity. She felt as disconnected from these events as she had felt before the crime-scene tape went up. But the longer lasting and more virulent the public outrage became, the more detached and confused Rose became. The virus had gone away. She was a good person. And she was as genuinely appalled as everyone else by speculative descriptions of the monster who must have done this dreadful thing in the bush. Because it wasn't her.

Strangers began to demand answers and action. There were neither. A police psychologist was interviewed in an air-conditioned studio and even in the crisp heat of the bush fringe, trying and failing to offer something other than a tabloid sound bite to the fray. An appeal for the mother to come forward. There were grave concerns for her mental and physical health. The mother needed help and compassion. She shouldn't be afraid to reach out for support.

Rose's eyes grew leaden with sadness as she watched the psychologist squinting into the camera so she squinted back, narrowing her eyes until their furrowed aperture was wet and foggy.

"Isn't it so sad, Mother," she said.

Violet scoured the newspapers and watched every news bulletin. She became snappy and non-communicative. She cried throughout a church sermon for the Baby in the Bush, as if her own heart were buried with it.

Rose sat beside her mother and watched a thick stalactite of mucus crawl unnoticed from Violet's nostril to her upper lip. Rose was fascinated by it. She had never seen her mother cry in church before. So Rose reached across and took her mother's hand and gave it a small squeeze of support.

Violet turned and looked at her daughter, looked at the small smile of sympathy on Rose's face, felt the gentle press of Rose's fingers around her own, and cried even harder.

Michael's family was in church too, but Rose noticed that Michael wasn't. His family sat, a slightly smaller but nonetheless cohesive group, moving in unison with the rest of the congregation: sit, stand, kneel, stand, sit. Rose couldn't help but think they were like a school of fish, ducking and weaving with a fluid and practiced unanimity.

The image made her smile. She didn't realize she was the only one in the church not moving in accord.

Michael hadn't returned any of Rose's calls or texts, so Rose stopped sending them. That urgent need she had initially felt to speak to him had dissipated. She existed now behind a thick pane of glass, present but unnoticeably separate from everyone around her. She knew she could exist in this state forever. Her insides were finally quiet. She wondered if it showed.

It showed to Liv. Liv saw Rose sinking into a hole with a ghost in her arms and there was absolutely nothing she could do about it.

Liv was walking through the mall one afternoon when she first heard it. She was accustomed to hearing things muttered by one particular group of girls whenever she walked by. Liv would muster up something equally cutting and witty with which to engage them — not because she cared what they thought, but because it gave her genuine pleasure.

Liv was unprepared, however, for what she heard this day. And her lack of preparation disarmed her completely.

She was almost adjacent to the group when she heard Louise Wright say, "Baby killer."

At first Liv thought she had misheard. She slowed her stride just enough to catch the second hiss of it, from two girls this time, slightly out of sync so the words bit into each other in a murmured counterpoint.

"Filthy baby killer."

Liv stopped and turned to face the group. Small smiles and solid stances told her they knew they had her. She felt her feet shifting slightly beneath her, willed herself not to shuffle them about. Felt a tingle in her extremities.

Said, "What did you say?"

"You heard," Louise said. Murmurs of solidarity. The group moved and responded like a military unit. They even had a uniform, all labels and lip gloss. They were as relaxed and confident in this moment as Liv was restless.

Liv hated Louise Wright, had laughed in her face many times with the knowledge that being high-school royalty did not translate in the real world. Two months out of school, when this girl was first slapped down by a real-life situation, she would probably crumble in confusion that she was not respected for no other reason than that she simply existed.

Louise continued, "Everyone knows. Everyone's talking about it."

Two steps closer to Liv. Flank following.

"It was only a matter of time before you squeezed one

out, slut. And what were you going to do? Live happily ever after with the baby-daddy? Oh, wait. It'd be impossible to figure out who that is, wouldn't it, bike?"

Giggles of camaraderie from the pack followed by perfectly timed support.

"Yeah."

"Right."

Louise moved in close and whispered, "Did you kill it before you buried it? Or did it die inside you out of sickness at having to share a body with you?"

Liv put months of staying-out-of-it into the slap that followed. She smacked Louise with such force and speed that there was a moment of shocked silence before the bawling began.

Liv's hand was stinging. Louise squatted on the floor howling, tears burning the perfectly forming impression of Liv's open palm. The knot of supporters with the collapsed princess dropped to their knees around her in unison, easing her into a sitting position as strangers began to gather.

Liv walked away, legs shaking, as a horrified shopper began talking about finding the security personnel.

30

Liv sat on her bed hugging her knees, head down, while her mother lay on the end of the bed, elbow crooked, head resting on one hand.

"You're going to tell me to stay out it," Liv said matter-of-factly.

"Yes," her mum replied. "Yes, I am."

Liv had come home crying, a large bruise beginning to swell on the heel of her hand.

Her mother made her a cup of tea and listened, and just when Liv thought they had reached the same impasse of denial and non-involvement, her mum said, "I do want you to stay out of it. But I'm not."

Liv looked up then.

Her mother gave a small smile and continued, "The police called."

"Why would they call you?"

"I gave my details at the hospital when I took Rose in. The hospital must have contacted them. Put two and two together. I knew it was only a matter of time."

"Will you get in trouble?" Liv asked. She felt strangely

relieved, even with the dread of her mother getting into trouble making her feel sick with guilt. She closed her eyes against a sudden dry stinging. The air in the room was giving her a headache. She hadn't realized how tired she was.

"I don't think so," her mother continued. "Plausible deniability, isn't that what they call it? Oh, and we did save that stupid girl's life." She rolled onto her back then and started talking at the ceiling. "They would have talked to Violet by now. Did I tell you Violet called me before I had a chance to call her? She was all over this. Thanked me for taking her daughter to the hospital when she fell ill. *Fell ill.* Poor Violet."

"Poor Violet?" Liv said doubtfully.

Liv's mum rolled onto her stomach and shimmied around to face her daughter. She reached out a hand and rested it on Liv's foot before continuing.

"I'm going to go in and talk to the police. They haven't asked me to yet but they will. And I don't want you to take the blame. I really don't want some group of acrylic-nailed, push-up bra vigilantes waiting for you in a carpark somewhere."

Liv closed her hand into a fist, then slowly released each finger, feeling the throb of the developing bruise deep in the plump pad of tissue at the base of her thumb. It felt good to manipulate it.

"When will you go to the police?"

Liv's mother didn't answer immediately, and when she did she caught Liv by surprise by saying, "It's a sort of madness, you know." Then, "I'll go tomorrow."

"What?" Liv asked.

Liv's mum shook her head. She sat up and began swinging the pendant around her neck in ever-widening circles.

Then she said, "When I was a kid I had this dog that got hit by a car. Did I ever tell you that? I'd taken it out for a walk and it got away from me, ran onto the road. At first I thought it was all right. It was limping but it was keeping up. It was a long walk home. But by the time we got there the dog had sort of swelled up and it wasn't walking right. My dad said it was probably bleeding internally, so he put it in the car and drove away. When he came back the dog wasn't with him. And we never talked about it. Nobody said to me, 'We had to have the dog put to sleep.' Nobody said a word. The dog was just gone, as if it had never been there."

"What was the dog's name?" Liv asked.

"I was too little to be walking that dog alone. I wasn't supposed to. I couldn't control it if it decided to piss off, which is exactly what it did. So I pretended it had never happened, because that's what everyone else was doing."

Liv didn't know what to say. She watched her mother's pendant spiraling in the light, the tiny bell at its center purring through the arcs. It was Liv's favorite.

"Do you know," her mum continued, "I don't even remember that goddamn dog's name."

31

That smoky light that always bloomed before sunrise itself was beginning to settle on Rose's windowpane. It wasn't really light so much as the shallow end of the night stretching translucent arms into the moments before day.

Rose had always liked the color of this predawn air. It was the color of a spider's web. Layers of dark kept being peeled away, real morning light creeping over treetops and buildings to find people's openings.

Rose felt her eyes adjusting, felt her pupils narrow with an aperture-like whir, and wondered if the light was encroaching or the dark receding. The transition from one to the other seemed very smooth first thing in the morning and late in the afternoon. They just bled into each other.

Rose had decided to stay in bed all day. She was unaware of the process that had led to that decision. She had been having trouble making decisions lately.

It wasn't even really a decision. It was more a conclusion that had simply landed on her and stuck. It came from far away, this desire to remain motionless, thoughtless, speechless. She didn't think she could raise her head from the pillow.

It only seemed like five minutes later that she heard people at the front door. When she opened her eyes, though, the light in the room was high and polished, so she must have slept for a while. Rose could hear her mother and father talking to other people, and sometimes her mother's voice rose into that frightened, resolute chirrup.

They were coming down the hall. Those voices were all getting closer, like a marching band that began two blocks away and was about to pass right by.

Except it didn't pass by.

Rose heard her mother say, "She has been unwell!" before the door opened and the band arrived.

Then there were two police officers in her bedroom. A man and a lady.

Rose's mother walked quickly to the side of her bed and said, "These people would like to talk to you, Rosie."

Rose sat up, bringing her knees to her chest, just as her phone rang.

She went to reach for it. It was Liv.

That's when the lady police officer stepped forward and said, "Do you mind if we have a talk before you answer that, Rose?"

And she said it in such a pleasant, firm way that Rose let the phone ring out and go to voicemail.

The pleasant, firm lady continued, "Rose? We were wondering if you would mind getting dressed and coming with us for a while. Your mum and dad have said it's okay and they can come too."

"Okay," Rose said.

Rose looked at her mother and managed a trembling smile.

That's when she saw it. The thing that had started in her mother's bones that day in the hospital, that mixture of shame and fear that both paralyzed and motivated in varying and conflicting degrees, had crawled right through her and landed, in this moment, on her face louder than a scream.

Rose hadn't asked why the pleasant, firm police lady wanted to talk to her.

Rose knew immediately that something had changed forever between all of them but she didn't care. It was strangely comforting, this disconnection.

The band stepped into the hall and gently pulled the door to without fully closing it. They were waiting for her to get dressed.

She didn't want to keep them waiting but couldn't make a decision about what to wear. It was hot in this room, and probably much hotter outside.

Rose peeled a shift dress off her floor and pulled it over her head. She could only find one sandal and the frustration of it almost defeated her.

She sat heavily on the edge of her bed.

"Are you almost ready, Rose?"

A different voice now, the man from the other side of the door, from the other side of everything.

Rose could hear them all whispering to each other.

"Just a minute," Rose said. She dropped to her knees to look in the only place she hadn't for her missing sandal. Under the bed.

That's when she saw it. The gym bag. Pushed against the wall, its shiny surface dulled by a patina of dust.

She leaned in and grabbed one handle, then gently

dragged it towards her.

"We have to go now, Rose." Nice lady again. And the door slowly eased open.

Rose was kneeling on the floor by her bed gripping the gym bag.

She looked up and said, "Can I bring this with me?"

Her mother was crying. Her father extended a tentative hand towards Violet as if to comfort her, but dropped it to his side again before contact was made.

When the doorbell finished its final diminuendo, Michael's father walked down the hall in purposeful strides and swung the front door open without a moment's hesitation. It was one fluid movement, one arm extending towards the doorknob before he reached the door, the other spontaneously straightening his tie.

The last sound of the bell was still resonating in Michael's head and the house when Michael realized how odd it was for his father to be wearing a tie when he was at home.

The door was opened and Michael listened to his father's perfectly clipped consonants ricochet off the cornices just as the doorbell had.

Everyone knew that tone. The tone that accompanied the tie. Michael and Tim had often laughed about their father's tie-tone. It was his voice for outsiders.

Two police officers stepped across the threshold looking purposeful yet somehow apologetic. There were handshakes. Michael watched from his perch on the arm of a lounge chair. Ludicrously, he waited for his father to introduce him to the outsiders.

Then it occurred to him that they knew who he was and that's why they were here.

For just a moment he let himself imagine and believe that they were here because they had discovered he was one of the ring-barking culprits. But that didn't wash.

He stood up and waited, feeling sick and wanting to cry, feeling the burn of tears backwashing into a salty swallow. He realized then he had no idea where his mother was.

He hadn't been following the conversation between his father and the police. Panic had bunged his ears. Had there been a conversation?

Suddenly all three were standing in front of Michael and someone had their hand on his shoulder saying, "You'll have to come with us for a bit, Mike," and the shock of hearing the unfamiliar abbreviation of his name snapped him back into the present moment at the same time that Tim opened the front door.

Tim stepped forward, the big loop of his keychain hooked onto one finger, the hand forming a fist.

He said the first words Michael actually heard completely clearly.

"Michael, are you okay?"

"Tim, this is not your business," his father said.

The police were leading Michael towards the front door. Tim had to step aside to let them pass.

He said to Michael, "I'll be right behind you."

"No, you won't," was his father's response.

"You're not making him go alone?" Tim asked.

He looked from his father to Michael to the police and

back to his father. The police led Michael outside. One of them held Michael's upper arm. Michael was listing slightly, and it appeared as if he might tip over without the restrained grip of the officer fastened above his elbow.

"Dad, please!" Tim said.

"He's eighteen," his father said, adjusting his tie slightly. Tim noticed that his father's hand was shaking. "He doesn't need ... babysitting." This last word after a slight pause.

Then, turning to face Tim and standing close, "And don't think I haven't noticed that you haven't asked why the police are here."

Tim knew then it was all falling apart and that he, his dad, his mum, were about to become a part of the human debris.

His father walked away, loosening his tie. Tim realized his car keys were digging into his palm and so he threw them onto the coffee table. He knew his mother wasn't home. He knew because this front room was awash with light. On hot days his mother always shut the house up against the heat. That's what she called it.

"We have to shut up against the heat," she would say, running about first thing in the morning closing windows, snapping blinds shut, drawing curtains and sometimes even securing the drops in the center with a peg.

But this morning the light was barreling through the panes. A wedge of luminous sun fell across the carpet sharp as a knife, bringing glare and dusty heat.

Tim found being caught in this strident light quite shocking.

It didn't take a lot of thought. He grabbed his car keys off the coffee table and ran out the front door, letting it slam behind him.

32

The first thing Rose noticed was the Christmas decorations. There was a real tree in the entrance. They had a plastic one at home with threadbare branches that had to be placed in the holes in the trunk in the correct order. If you didn't stick them in the holes in the correct order then the tree didn't end up the right shape and had a tendency to tip over.

Rose couldn't stop looking at this one. It was thick and smelled luxurious. Instead of tinsel it had been draped with that bright yellow crime-scene tape.

Rose thought that was very funny. She smiled as she reached in through the needles, soft as hair, and pierced a sap blister on its knobby trunk with her thumbnail.

When she withdrew her hand, the sticky remnant's sharp perfume cleared her head like a slap in the face.

"What are you doing!" Violet wasn't asking. There was no question in it at all.

Rose rubbed the gummy tree blood between her thumb and forefinger and held it up to her mother's face.

"Can we have a real Christmas tree next time, Mum?"

Tim watched Rose sniffing her fingers from the other

side of the room in disbelief. It wasn't the oddness of her gesture but rather his shock at almost not recognizing her. He hadn't seen her for months and was unprepared for the vacuous caricature that presented itself at the reception desk with her mother and two police officers.

She was cadaverously thin, her facial bones stretching her skin like sharpened knuckles. It was as if the Rose he knew had somehow vanished, and her incremental return was only half done. The eyes weren't back. Not by a long shot.

Jesus Christ, did she just ask for a Christmas tree?

Michael had already been taken somewhere else. Somewhere inside. Somewhere in there behind the shiny formica desk adorned with a fringe of tinsel. They had asked Tim to wait here. They said he could see Michael soon. They asked if Michael's parents were coming.

The last thing Tim was able to say to Michael as he was maneuvered into the police car was, "Don't say anything!"

But Michael's eyes were closed and there was such a look of liberation on his face, Tim felt sickeningly worried that Michael had every intention of saying everything.

Rose saw Tim across the room and waved. It was a reflex, but a genuine pleasantry nonetheless.

She was confused by his reaction. He looked appalled.

Violet grabbed her hand as it flailed the paltry greeting and yanked it down to her side. She kept holding it.

Rose said, "You're hurting my hand, Mum."

Violet continued to grip Rose's hand as they were shown to seats and asked to wait. Violet was not usually overly demonstrative, so this hand-holding was embarrassing and irritating to Rose. There didn't seem to be much affection in it. Rose tried to flex her fingers against the restrictive heat of her mother's consistent palm pressure.

It was too hot in here. She couldn't breathe. It felt as if her lungs rather than her fingers were in her mother's grip. She tried to pull her hand away and found her mother countering with surprising force.

Tim watched this struggle, a strange arm wrestle, and rooted for Violet. Because if Rose waved at him again he just might cross the room and cuff her across the side of the head.

Rose wondered if the air conditioning in here was working. Her head was foggy. She heard her phone ringing from a long way away and found it difficult to focus on the screen.

It was Liv. She was going to answer it but her mother reached across and took the phone from her, pocketing it deftly without once releasing her grip on Rose.

It didn't matter because Liv walked through the door then, her phone pressed to the side of her head. She paused briefly before striding across to Rose and landing heavily on the seat beside her.

She nodded towards the Christmas tree in the entrance and said, "Police tape? Really? That's fucking poor taste."

Violet leaned across Rose and said, "Hello, Liv. How are you, dear?"

Tim watched Rose, defined and sheltered by seconds, and thought about Michael alone somewhere in there behind these clean lines and quiet voices that were disturbingly welcoming.

That's when he saw the two police officers walk across to Rose's united front.

He immediately stood and walked across, himself.

"Rose, we'd like you to come with us and answer a few questions. Your mum can come with you if you like."

"Is she under arrest?" Liv asked.

"Yes, is she under arrest?" Tim said. "And can I see my brother now?"

"Michael's here?" Rose asked. "Where's Michael?"

"Yes, Michael's here, you stupid bitch."

"Sir, we're going to have to insist that you take your seat again."

"Don't talk to her like that," Liv said. "Don't you fucking talk to her at all."

"Don't talk to her? That's my brother in there!"

"Oh please, oh please." Violet sang it like a hymn, eyes trained squarely on the carpet.

"Take your seat now, sir. I'm not going to ask again."

One of the officers stepped forward and placed himself between Tim and Liv.

Rose stood then and found herself anchored by hand-holding on either side. Liv gave Rose's hand a final squeeze and then released it.

Rose and Violet were led through a door to a long corridor freckled with bulletin boards. It seemed to go on forever. There were glass-walled offices to the left. There were people behind the glass, standing at desks as if to attention, watching Rose as she walked past.

It was like a zoo, except Rose was the exhibit. She began to feel claustrophobic.

That's when she saw him, walking towards her from the other end of the enclosure.

Rose hesitated for just a second, her blood galumphing through a pulse roll that smacked her senses wide open. She felt like she had that first day on the beach.

Frightened and exhilarated, she watched Michael get closer, recognized his relaxed gait, saw his face ease open as he approached her.

What Rose saw on him was relief. He wore it like a skin.

They calculated each other's approach and positioned themselves such that one would drag their fingers across the back of the other's. Somehow this small gesture had more significance than the usual body-slam hugging that had been their previous mid-hall greeting.

As his fingers grazed hers, he turned briefly to her and said, "We're almost there, Rose."

ACKNOWLEDGMENTS

I very much want to thank Erica Wagner for believing in this book from the beginning and providing such consistent support and guidance. I also want to thank Sophie Splatt, my editor, for some cracking insights and for putting up with me. And I must thank Joscelyn Evans — friend, confidante, critic, voice of reason, reality check and the only person who gets to read the first draft.

ABOUT THE AUTHOR

After living in the US for ten years, Dianne Touchell now resides in Perth, Australia. Her first novel, *Creepy & Maud*, was shortlisted for the Children's Book Council of Australia's Book of the Year Award. She has worked as a fish-and-chip-shop counter girl, nightclub singer, housekeeper and bookseller. She enjoys school visits and encouraging teenagers to consider reading and writing for pleasure as an outlet for the secret madness that is life on this planet. She has also published poetry and short stories and is a member of the Australian Society of Authors.